SEARCHING FOR LOVE

"I know I'm starting to sound like a broken record," Mike said, "but are you sure your mom's okay? I have a feeling you're not telling me something."

Deni turned her face toward her window. "Why are you trying to make me feel guilty?"

"I'm not."

"Yes, you are. Or else why would you keep bringing her up when we're here searching for my real mother?"

"Your *real* mother is back in Topeka," he snapped, anger in his voice. "The mother you owe your loyalty and love to is not the person you're trying to find today."

Deni stared out the window, blinking back sudden tears. She had never heard him use this tone of voice before. Why was he trying to get her to back out at the last minute by making her feel guilty? Why didn't he understand?

Bantam Sweet Dreams Romances
Ask your bookseller for the books you have missed

Searching for Love

Andrea Warren

BANTAM BOOKS
TORONTO • NEW YORK • LONDON • SYDNEY • AUCKLAND

RL 6, IL age 11 and up

SEARCHING FOR LOVE
A Bantam Book / July 1987

Sweet Dreams and its associated logo are registered trademarks
of Bantam Books, Inc. Registered in U.S. Patent and Trademark
Office and elsewhere.

Cover photo by Pat Hill.

ISBN 0-553-26292-0

Published simultaneously in the United States and Canada

Bantam Books are published by Bantam Books, Inc. Its trademark,
consisting of the words "Bantam Books" and the portrayal of a
rooster, is Registered in U.S. Patent and Trademark Office and in
other countries. Marca Registrada, Bantam Books, Inc., 666 Fifth
Avenue, New York, New York 10103.

Reproduced, printed and bound in Great Britain by
Hazell Watson & Viney Limited,
Member of the BPCC Group,
Aylesbury, Bucks

Searching for Love

Chapter One

Denise Lambert ran lightly down the stairs, glancing out the window on the landing as she passed it. The weather report on the radio had been right! she thought. The morning sun shone brightly. The long stretch of gray, rainy days was over.

Deni opened the front door and stepped onto the porch, shivering in the cool morning air. Roses were in full bloom by the steps. Overhead, birds flew from branch to branch in the trees. She hugged herself. Anything was possible on such a perfect day!

She danced back into the house and into the sunny, peach-colored kitchen and gave her mother a quick kiss on the cheek.

"Morning, honey," Mrs. Lambert said. "You're certainly full of energy today! I like the dress," she added approvingly, looking at Deni. "You made a good purchase with your first paycheck."

"Thanks, Mom!" Deni twirled around the kitchen and startled Sam, her cat. He was seated by his food bowl, waiting for breakfast. As Deni approached he scampered out of her way. "And I get paid again today, so I think I'll stop at Macy's on the way home. The junior department is having a sale. I *love* having a job and making money!" she declared.

Deni peered into the skillet at the mixture her mother was stirring. "Ugh, scrambled eggs? Really, Mother!" She put the back of her hand to her forehead and rolled her eyes dramatically. "*Must* we start out an otherwise beautiful summer morning with something that's yellow and yucky?"

"Eggs are good for you. I would have made an omelet but I want to get to work a little early today," Mrs. Lambert said. She scooped the eggs onto two plates.

Deni sighed resignedly and poured orange juice into the glasses on the table. "Scrambled, fried, poached, whatever. I hate breakfast, so what I eat really doesn't matter," she said.

"You're just like your father was," her mother scolded gently. "John always wanted to get in at least two hours of work before he thought about food. I just can't agree with that. Everyone needs a good breakfast before the day's work begins."

Deni watched her mother closely as she spoke. John Lambert, Deni's father, had died six years before in an automobile accident. It

2

was only in the last year that her mother had been able to mention his name without starting to cry. Now when she referred to him in conversation, Deni heard only fondness in her voice, not pain.

Mrs. Lambert put the plates of food on the table and sat down. "Don't forget to start saving part of your paycheck this week. Remember you can buy clothes and records, as long as you cover your expenses, like gasoline."

Deni swallowed a sip of juice. "No problem, Mom," she said. "I'm working out a budget, just like I told you I would. I'll show it to you when I get finished. Why are you going to work early?" she asked, to change the subject. She had never had to manage money before. Her first paycheck, which she had received the week before, was already spent, and she still had a long list of things she wanted to buy.

Mrs. Lambert buttered her toast. "We have a big meeting at the office this morning. The foundation is getting involved in some new research, and my division will handle the project funding. Early morning is the only time we can get everyone together. Oh, by the way, are you going over to your grandmother's today?"

Deni nodded. She reached for the jam jar and spread a generous layer of blackberry preserves on her toast. Eight days ago her grandmother had suffered chest pains. The doctor had suspected that she had experienced a minor heart attack, but he had allowed her to remain at home instead of being hospitalized. She had to rest most of the time. Deni and Mrs. Lambert were assuming most of the care of her home and yard and also were keeping her company as much as possible. Deni had been spending each afternoon with her grandmother, driving there directly from her part-time job at a television station.

"Can you do some weeding today? The flower beds are getting out of control with all the rain we've had. Mother mentioned the daisies yesterday. It bothers her not to be able to keep them up the way she always has," Mrs. Lambert said.

"OK. I'll take my swimsuit along. I'll start on my suntan as I work on the flower beds," Deni replied. "It will save me from going to Macy's and spending all my money."

Deni watched her mother butter a second piece of toast. She never understood how Mrs. Lambert could eat such a large breakfast every day and still stay so slim. Her mother looked elegant and professional in a summer linen-weave gray suit that was one of Deni's favorites. It always surprised her to think that her mother was fifty-two years old. She was as much as ten years older than the mothers of some of Deni's friends, yet her age never bothered Deni.

"Got any special plans for the weekend?" her mother asked, smiling.

Deni shrugged. "I don't know. I might go to the sailing regatta at the lake tomorrow with

Jana or Kris. Or else I'll just take my sketch-book and go alone. It's really a drag without Lori here."

Sometimes she wondered how she was going to get through the rest of the summer without her best friend Lori. She had left the day after school was out to spend the summer in California with her father and new stepmother and live in the fishing camp they ran.

"I miss her, too," her mother said. "It always seemed like she spent as much time here as she did at her house. Is she getting along OK?"

"I guess so. She sounds pretty happy in her letters. Her stepmother's not bad. Just *young*," Deni said, laughing. "Did I tell you she's only twenty-two? Lori said they look the same age and people think they're sisters. I don't think she thinks its as great as her stepmother does."

Mrs. Lambert smiled. "That would be strange. I suppose Lori's got at least one boy-friend by now."

"Well, she's got him all picked out. His name is Scott. He and his parents came to the camp last week to stay for a month."

"Well, she'll be back before you know it," her mother said. "At least you've got your job at the television station to keep you busy, and—"

"Oh!" Deni said suddenly. "I almost forgot to tell you! I'm giving my first tour this morning. Roberta is gone today, and we have a

5

group of junior high kids from a summer class coming in."

"Kids?" Her mother looked amused. "You're not that much older than they are, my dear young lady."

"I *am* just a year away from college, Mom."

"You're growing up so fast. I can hardly believe I had to buy you a car," her mother mused.

"And do I love it!" Deni said. "Lori flipped out when I told her." Deni still couldn't believe it—a car of her very own! It was a shiny yellow compact Volkswagen, with a black interior, and a good radio. She poured herself another glass of juice. "Did Chuck tell you what he's working on now?" she asked, referring to her brother, who was program manager at the TV station. Chuck was ten years older than Deni. He had been married three years, and his wife, Kara, was expecting a baby in two months. Deni wondered if her mother and grandmother weren't more excited about the baby than the parents were.

"He hasn't said anything. Eat your breakfast, honey. It's getting cold. Does he have a new project?" Mrs. Lambert asked.

Deni absently stirred the eggs on her plate with her fork, trying to phrase her thoughts carefully. She hesitated, afraid that her voice would sound unnatural. "He's started a series on special children who are up for adoption," she said slowly, emphasizing the last word. "You know—kids with handicaps and stuff. The camera crew went out yesterday to start shooting." Deni looked right at her mother.

"Sounds interesting," Mrs. Lambert said guardedly. She sipped her coffee, avoiding her daughter's eyes. "Chuck has always had a soft spot for needy children. I remember when he was a little boy he was always collecting soda pop bottles and giving the money away to kids who had less."

Deni kept her voice even and unemotional. "I was sort of hoping he'd ask me to help with the story. Maybe I could talk to the kids a little to get them to open up." She paused, her eyes on her plate. "It might help if I told them *I'm* adopted."

Deni waited silently, unable to look at her mother. The fact that she had been adopted was something that she and her mother had never been able to discuss easily. She hadn't brought it up in a long time.

"Maybe he will," her mother said, her voice tight, her eyes downcast. Deni knew her mother didn't want to pursue the subject. Deni decided to change the subject. She knew there was no point in causing trouble before they both had to leave for work. Some other time would be better.

"Well, you know Chuck," Deni said lightly. "He never asks for my advice or help on anything. He still thinks he has to act like my father instead of my brother. *And* you'd think he's the only guy in the whole world who is about to become a father." She finished off her juice, noticing her mother's quick smile at the mention of Chuck facing fatherhood. "If *that* isn't bad enough," Deni continued, "since *he* got me my summer job, he has the nerve to act like my boss sometimes. When is he going to figure out that I'm practically grown-up? I think he needs to be reminded that I'm going to be a senior in high school next fall."

"I know how you must feel." Her mother's voice was sympathetic. "But try to bear with him. He feels responsible for all of us—Kara, you, me, and your grandmother. He still subscribes to the notion that the man of the family is supposed to look out for everyone. Even though," she added, a bemused look on her face, "*we* all know better. But you have to admit, it's nice having him around."

"Good old Chuck," Deni said fondly. She started to clear the table. "Once the baby is born—on August eighth, my seventeenth birthday, of course—then maybe he'll forget about tormenting his poor little kid sister. Do you know that at work he actually has the nerve to tell people we're related? Sometimes I think I'm going to die of embarrassment."

"I'm sure he doesn't know it's embarrassing for you," her mother said, laughing. "He's proud of you. But I'll mention it to him, if you want me to." She gave Deni a quick hug. "Is work going well otherwise?"

Deni shrugged. "It's OK. Nothing special. I can hardly complain when I'm lucky enough to have a part-time job. Let's just say I am definitely not going to be a receptionist when

I grow up. Boring, boring, boring! I'll be a station manager instead."

"I certainly hope so! Or a career in art would be nice." Her mother began to rinse dishes and put them in the dishwasher. "Which reminds me—did you give the drawing to Mr. Robbins?"

Deni's face lit up. Her mother was referring to a sketch of the TV station that Deni had drawn for her boss. "Yes! He liked it so much he showed it to Chuck, and now Chuck wants one." She put her eggs down the garbage disposal before her mother could protest. "Next summer I want to help film and edit stories. I like being in the studio, but I don't ever get back there unless I have a phone message to deliver to someone. Do you think Chuck could help me get a studio job?"

"You don't have any experience. But maybe you could get into the student internship program." Her mother looked at her with interest, a smile on her face. "Your sudden interest in television production doesn't have anything to do with a certain camera intern, does it?" she asked teasingly.

"Of course not," Deni said with mock indignation. She felt her cheeks get hot. "How could you even *think* such a thing!"

"Seems like I've been hearing the name Mike Hogan rather often since you started your job. And I think I do detect a bit of blush on m'lady's cheeks at the mention of his name."

"What *I* think is that it's time you got to work, Mom," Deni said, nudging her mother out of the kitchen. "I'll finish up here and feed Sam. You said you wanted to leave a little early today. Bye! See you at supper!"

Deni went and stood at the sink and waved through the window as her mother backed her car out of the garage onto the wide, two-car driveway. Then she reached up into the cupboard and took a can of cat food out and opened it. Sam meowed loudly, rubbing his chubby body against her leg. "Patience, patience, my fat friend," she said as she filled his bowl on the counter. "At least you don't have to struggle through scrambled eggs. If you ask me, your Fisherman's Delight looks better than what I had for breakfast." She switched the radio from the news station her mother liked to listen to and found a local rock station. One of her favorite songs was playing, and she began to dance around the kitchen. Sam ambled over to the place where his food bowl should have been. Deni picked him up and hugged him.

"It's a beautiful day, Sam," Deni said happily. "Just look at that sunshine! In one half hour I'll be at the station, and I just have a feeling that today I'm going to see Mike. Green eyes, just like yours. Only you have yellow fur, and he's got gorgeous short, light brown hair. Otherwise," she said, touching her nose to the cat's, "the two of you look a lot alike. But how can I get him to ask me out? What do you think, Sam?" The cat avoided her stare and looked longingly at the food in his dish on the counter instead. "Should I ask him out? Lots of girls ask guys out. Just because I never have doesn't mean it isn't time for a first." She swung the cat around with her as she danced to the music. "It's possible, of course, that he thinks I'm too young for him. Or too ugly, or—"

Deni caught a glimpse of herself in the kitchen mirror. Her shiny dark brown hair, loosely curled, just touched the top of her shoulders. She had tied a light yellow ribbon in it to match her new oxford-cloth dress, setting off her dark brown eyes and clear skin. She was wearing her new frosted coral lipstick, which, along with a little bit of blush, added subdued color to her face.

"No, not too ugly," Deni said to her reflection. "Definitely not too ugly." She tried out several poses in front of the mirror. Sam struggled to be let down, and she finally set him on the floor and gave him his food dish. She looked in the mirror again and batted her thick, dark brown eyelashes. "Knock him dead, kid," she said in a low whisper to her reflection. "He'll be putty in your hands."

She glanced at the clock. She had twenty minutes before it was time to leave for work. From her purse she took out the half-finished letter she had written to Lori the night before and sat down at the table to scan it.

She hadn't gotten very far because she didn't like sitting down and concentrating on one task, but for Lori she made an exception. They had been best friends since junior high, and in the fall they had arranged to take

French and social issues together. They had promised to write each other at least every other day while Lori was gone. For a moment Deni chewed on the end of her pen, then wrote down "Friday" so Lori would know it was a new section:

I have my new dress on. I think it looks good. Today is sunny! I called Carol B. last night to ask if she knew Mike when she went to Harding High, and she said she knew who he was but she didn't know if he had a girlfriend. I wish I could find out. Try to think of someone else I can ask. I still think I've seen him somewhere with someone we know. Carol said he was a photographer for the school paper, and she said she always thought he was cute.

Deni had seen Mike on her second day of work when she had to deliver a phone message to the studio. (She had already written Lori the details of that first encounter.) He had smiled at her, and they then exchanged names. She had learned that he was going to be a freshman at the University of Kansas in the fall and was an intern at the station for the summer. They had been interrupted before they could talk further, and since then, even though she had been at the station for two full weeks, she had only seen him from a distance.

Deni debated whether or not to tell Lori that she had brought up the subject of adoption with her mother that morning. But Lori wasn't especially comfortable with the topic, either. Every time Deni brought it up Lori acted stiff and peculiar. Deni sighed. Adoption was one subject she couldn't talk to anyone about. Chuck had never shown any interest, and her grandmother's reaction was only slightly better than her mother's. Sometimes she wondered if they were trying to hide something from her about her past. The little bit of information her mother had given her was so sketchy: "The woman who gave birth to you was eighteen when she put you up for adoption. She wasn't married." That was the end of the subject.

Deni stared at the paper. She needed to finish the letter and get to work. She told Lori how nervous she was about giving her first tour, but she decided not to mention how much she was hoping to see Mike. Finally she added a note about her grandmother's recovery and signed off.

Deni quickly read through the finished letter, then sealed it and addressed the envelope. She missed Lori so much! Ever since Lori had left for California, Deni had been sticking close to home or spending her time with her grandmother or Kara. Her mother had commented that Deni seemed to prefer the company of adults to people her own age. Deni had to admit that she did enjoy being around adults, especially Kara. Chuck's wife was like a sister to her.

Yet Lori was still her very best friend, and Deni would have to get through the rest of the summer without her. They had already talked about going to the same college together and being roommates.

Deni glanced at the clock. Twenty after eight. She turned off the radio and grabbed her purse.

"Bye, Sam," she said, scratching his head. "I'm off to pursue my career in television. *And* to pursue the boy of my dreams, but don't tell anyone. I'll fill you in this noon on everything that happens, you lucky cat!"

Deni glanced in the mirror one more time, then locked the back door and strode toward her car. The same feeling of anticipation she had felt earlier swept over her once again. Something wonderful was going to happen— she just knew it.

Chapter Two

The clock on the wall said exactly 8:30 when Deni slid into the chair behind the receptionist's desk. She slipped her purse in a drawer, turned the calendar to the right date, then picked up the ringing phone.

"Channel Twenty-one, Topeka," she said cheerfully.

"When is that show on—you know the one—that one with that boat in it?" asked the voice at the other end of the line. It sounded like an old man.

"Boat?" Deni hesitated. " 'The Love Boat?' "

"Yeah, that's the one. I can't remember the time."

"Every day at three-thirty," she said. "Thank you for calling."

A salesman came into the station and approached her desk. "Mr. Robbins isn't in yet," she said politely. "But you can either wait here or outside his office."

"Thank you, miss. I'll just stay put," he said in a friendly tone. He sat down in one of the chairs. The phone rang just then. Deni answered it, and a secretary at another station asked her for scheduling information. While she was looking it up, Mr. Robbins came in, nodded at her, and ushered the salesman into his office.

It was fun having Roberta away, Deni thought. It meant she could do things like give the tour, handle the phone calls, and greet salespeople. What did Roberta do when it got busy and she was alone? Deni hoped she wouldn't have to find out. She turned her attention back to her work and started to double-check a stack of program sheets and date them. When she was just finishing them, she looked up and discovered Chuck standing in front of her, smiling down.

"Hi, Sis." A coffee cup in his hand, he sat down in the chair beside her desk. He was tall and very blond, with blue eyes and an athletic build. He always dressed casually in slacks and light sweaters, and to Deni, he looked as if he would be more at home at a country club than at a television station. "How's Mom?" he asked.

"Seems fine," Deni replied. "Important meeting at the foundation this morning, but, of course, we found time to have a big breakfast." She rolled her eyes, and Chuck laughed.

"That's Mom for you. 'If you eat good food, you'll have a good day.' But I'm just like her about breakfast. You're—"

"Like Daddy was. I know, I know. She keeps telling me that. I don't remember him *ever* getting out of eating what she put in front of him." She smiled at her brother. "So how's Kara doing?"

"Fatter than ever!" He grinned broadly. "She saw Dr. Hansen yesterday, and the baby kicked during the whole examination. Doc says it's a girl. He knows he's got a fifty-fifty chance of guessing right. She's had more aches and pains lately, but I guess that's natural. We started wallpapering the nursery last night. Why don't you stop over and see it?"

"I will. Kara showed me the paper last week. I *love* the idea of doing everything in teddy bears." She thought for a moment. "Maybe I can come over tomorrow. I'll be at Gram's all afternoon today."

"It's great of you to spend so much time there, Den. Mom and I sure appreciate it. Kara went over yesterday and said Grandmother looked pretty good."

Deni nodded. "She still has to rest an awful lot, though. She has two more tests scheduled for next week."

"She's just lucky Dr. Brock isn't insisting she stay in the hospital." Chuck frowned. "But it would probably kill her to have to leave her house, and I think he knows that. I'd stop by today, but we're taping another segment on our adoptive kids story."

"I can hardly wait to see it—is it going OK?"

"Real good." Chuck had a soft smile on his face. "The kids are incredible. That little boy we taped the other day—Freddie—was the greatest little guy. Three years old, mildly retarded, so sweet that you didn't want to do anything but hold him. I sure hope our story helps find a family for him. The adoption agency has been really cooperative. They take good care of the kids." The phone rang. Deni turned to answer it.

Chuck waited while she answered the phone. When she hung up, he cleared his throat and nervously twisted his wedding ring. Deni looked at him searchingly. She knew he was about to say something.

"Den," he finally asked, his voice serious, "does it ever bother you that you were adopted and I wasn't?"

Deni was surprised by his question and hesitated before answering it. He had never asked her anything like that before. Even though she had known she was adopted from the time she was old enough to understand what the word meant, she had learned long ago that it wasn't a subject to be discussed at home, even with Chuck.

Just as she had with her mother that morning, Deni weighed her words carefully before she spoke. "Not really," she said slowly. "You're so much older than I am that I can't say Mom and Daddy ever showed any favoritism—if that's what you mean."

"Now wait a minute!" He laughed. "Ten years isn't all that much older." His eyes softened as he looked at her. "I remember so well when they brought you home. I was a little jealous at first, but having you with us made everything more fun."

Deni tried not to show that she was touched by his words. Her mother was right: Chuck was a softie. He had always been a loving, protective big brother. But he was more of a big brother to her than a friend. She had always hoped that they would be able to ignore the age gap between them and talk to each other as equals. "I guess if I had to be adopted, I've turned out OK. I just wish—"

"What?" Chuck asked, looking at her earnestly.

"Well," she said carefully, "I've always wanted to know who my birth parents were. I know it sounds silly, but I always used to fantasize— when I was *little*," she added quickly, "that my mother was a glamorous movie star who was forced to give me up. You know, stories like that."

"I didn't know," Chuck said, a surprised look on his face. He sipped his coffee and studied her. "I never figured you thought much about any of it at all. At least it never seemed to bother you." He paused for a moment. "You knew enough to know that she couldn't have been famous."

"You mean because she was a teenager and wasn't married?" Deni asked. She shrugged. "Sure, I knew. But you can't tell a kid that. Kids think whatever they want."

What would Chuck think if she told him that she *still* had the fantasy sometimes that she was reunited with a rich, beautiful, loving, and generous woman who was her birth mother? Yet she rarely, if ever, thought about having a birth father. It was her mother she was curious about.

"I guess I can see what you're saying about a childhood fantasy," Chuck said. "But you don't really care anymore, do you?"

"Sure!" she said quickly. "For one thing, I'd like to know who I look like."

"But it doesn't matter—"

"Not to you, you *know* who you look like," she said defensively. "You're built like Daddy, and you have blond hair and blue eyes like Mom. One of these days you'll have gray hair like Mom," she said, wrinkling her nose at him. "But me—I look in the mirror and see dark brown hair, dark brown eyes, and I'm the only one in the family who has them. Daddy was tall, and so are you and Mom. I'm not. I just wonder who I look like. How they look now. How I'll look when I'm older. All of that."

Chuck looked alarmed at first, but then he became thoughtful. "Yeah, I can understand that." He gave her hand a squeeze. "For whatever it's worth, you do handle it very well. Nothing ever seems to bother you. You always have had lots of friends, Dad was crazy about you, Mom couldn't love you more—in fact, you and Mom always amaze me. You're more like best friends than mother and daughter."

Deni glanced at him from the corner of her eye. "As I was saying, I turned out OK for being adopted." What would he think if she told him that she found herself watching strangers at the shopping mall or on the streets, searching for a face like her own, a biological link to someone else in this world? Chuck was lucky. He had been almost an adult when their father died, and soon he would have a child of his own. He felt secure about his family. But not only was Deni adopted, she also had lost her adoptive father at age ten. For her, "family" was something fragmented.

"Uh-oh," she said, glancing outside the big glass front doors. "Here comes the junior high group for its tour. Talk to you later."

Chuck looked at the noisy thirteen- and fourteen-year-olds filing into the building, then got up quickly. "Good luck, kid," he said to her. "I'm going to make my escape while I can."

She dialed Mrs. Carter, the film librarian, to tell her to take over the incoming calls. Then she stood up and extended her hand to the teacher. "Hi, I'm Denise Lambert. I'm going to give you your tour."

He looked at her, surprised. "Are you new here? I remember an older woman giving tours," he said. "Roberta?"

Deni smiled. "She's out today. You're Mr. Dunlap?"

He nodded and shook her outstretched hand. "This is my summer English class. We're doing a media unit."

Deni smiled at the ten students standing

in front of her. Two boys, one with braces on his teeth, jabbed each other and grinned at her. "How old are you?" asked a short girl standing directly in front of her. "You don't look old enough to be doing this."

"Connie, please!" Mr. Dunlap pleaded. "Miss Lambert is obviously a professional." He was a thin man with nervous mannerisms. He smiled apologetically to Deni.

"I know my way around the studio," Deni said easily.

"Do you have a boyfriend?" asked the boy with braces. His friend howled in laughter and pretended to fall on the floor. Everybody giggled.

"Let's start over here," Deni said, ignoring his comment. She knew her face was flushed. "This first room on my right is the film library."

She showed them around, explaining how the library worked. As they looked around the room, she asked each of them their names. Rick, who had the braces, obviously liked her. He and the other boy, Dave, stayed together and followed Deni closely.

Several students asked questions. Connie asked the most. Mr. Dunlap seemed embarrassed by everything the students did or said and continually apologized for them to Deni.

The studio was their next stop. Deni started to get nervous. Mike was frequently out on assignment, so it was possible he wouldn't be there. But even though she had only talked to him once, she knew that she liked him.

Just the chance of talking to him again excited her.

It wasn't any specific thing that attracted Deni to him—it was *everything*—the cut of his light brown hair, his green eyes, his slender, wiry build. She liked the way he walked, the worn jeans and T-shirts he wore to work. And she liked his smile, she especially liked his smile. It was quick, friendly, and it lit up his face.

Deni knew so little about Mike, but she liked the intensity with which he approached his work. A few days before she had gone into the studio on an errand and secretly had watched him for several moments. She could tell he was concerned about every camera shot. Mike talked to people in a direct, attentive manner and listened to others the same way.

Deni wanted that attention focused on her. He was on her mind constantly.

As she led the class into the studio, she looked around quickly. Mike was there! Over in the corner with a cameraman named Keith, readying a camera for the noontime news. Her heart began to pound. She should have taken a minute to run a comb through her hair, she thought. But it was too late.

Deni stood with the little group in the middle of the studio, telling them about the preparation going on for the taping of the midday news. Keith caught her eye and signaled that he would show them the camera.

Her hands started to shake as Keith and Mike began to push it toward the group. The students swarmed around its base, eager to touch it and look through the sophisticated lens. Deni tried to focus on what Keith was saying. Mike was standing right next to him.

When each student began taking turns adjusting the viewscope, Mike moved over next to her. She felt breathless. She gave him a quick, polite smile and pretended to be absorbed in what the students were doing.

"I like the hair ribbon," he whispered. Her cheeks started to burn. Rick and Dave turned and stared at them and moved a step closer.

"Thanks," Deni whispered back, aware of the boy's curious eyes and the catch in her throat that kept the word from coming out smoothly. "I like your—your camera," she said lamely. How could she say something so stupid!

Mike chuckled softly. "So do I. This is one of the new ones. It's so sophisticated, it practically doesn't need anyone to operate it."

"Is that your boyfriend?" asked Rick loudly. Dave punched him in the side, and they started to laugh again. "Not since you got here, Rick," Deni said to him in a low, sweetly sarcastic voice that surprised her as much as it did him.

Dave exploded in laughter, causing the other students to stop and look at him. Rick blushed. Mike winked at Deni, then moved over to the other side of the camera to help Keith change its position. He was laughing, too. Mr. Dunlap started apologizing for everything.

* * *

During the next half hour, the students were very quiet and watched the taping of an interview to be shown on the noon news. They met the newscaster and watched one of the technicians touch up her makeup and put makeup on the man she was interviewing. Keith and Mike let each of them take turns standing behind the camera during the actual taping. The taping was still in session when Deni quietly led the students out of the studio so they could visit the film-editing room.

By the studio door Deni glanced back over her shoulder and saw Mike wave to her. She waved in return and then closed the door behind her. For a moment she stood in the hallway, tingling all over. He had complimented her on her hair ribbon, and then he had intentionally caught her eye as she was leaving!

As she was finishing the tour, Deni felt as if she were walking on clouds. She laughed and joked with the students, and when the tour was over, Deni was sorry to see them leave. She assured Mr. Dunlap that they were welcome to come back anytime.

The rest of the morning glowed from her encounter with Mike. As she worked quietly at her desk, completing some scheduling sheets, she relived every tiny detail of what they had said to each other. Something had to come out of that encounter—she was sure of it! But the waiting was so frustrating.

When it was time to leave, Deni put the

lunch-hour recording on the phone and readied things for Clara, the afternoon receptionist, who would be there at one o'clock. She worked slowly, reluctant to leave. She wouldn't be back until Monday, and a long weekend loomed ahead. The lobby was deserted. Mr. Robbins had already left for lunch.

Deni put her paycheck in her purse and then made a note to herself to stop by a toy store to find a teddy bear to take to Chuck and Kara for the nursery. As she opened the drawer where she kept her purse, she saw the sketch of the station she had started for Chuck and laid it on the desk so she could take it home and work on it over the weekend. She had just taken her car keys out of her purse when the hallway door that led to the studio opened.

"Hi," Mike said, stepping through the door. "I just wondered how you'd survived your first tour. It looked like you had everything and everyone under control."

"They were something!" she said, laughing nervously, the familiar burn returning to her cheeks. "Especially Rick—the kid with braces. I felt like I had a new puppy. Poor Mr. Dunlap—he doesn't seem like he's used to kids."

Mike's eyes fell on her sketch. "Did you do that?" he asked, picking it up. She nodded, embarrassed. "It's good. Do you do a lot of drawing?"

"I like to sketch, and I do some watercolor," she said shyly. "Buildings aren't my speciality. I like—" Something clicked in her brain, an idea that made her heart beat faster. "One thing I really like is boats. I live near Lake Shawnee, and there's a sailing regatta tomorrow. I'm going to ride my bike over and do some sketches. It's supposed to be a beautiful day." Would he take the hint?

Mike looked interested. "Do you like to sail?"

"I've never done it, to be honest. But I *think* I would. Do you?" Deni asked.

"Yes. I love it. My cousins have a small sailboat. So there's a regatta tomorrow, huh?"

Deni nodded. "Maybe," she said, summoning all the courage she had, "you'd like to take your camera, and we—"

"How did you know I like photography?" he asked, interrupting her and sounding surprised.

Deni blushed. "I know someone—Carol Bennett—who went to your school. I—we—just happened to be talking, and I mentioned that you worked here . . ."

Deni suddenly knew what it was like to die of embarrassment. She had been caught in the act of checking out Mike behind his back, just as she was in the process of asking *him* for a date. If only they could start the whole conversation over!

Mike was smiling at her. "I'll bring my camera—that's a great idea," he said enthusiastically. "What's your address? I'll put my bike on top of my car, and we can ride to the lake from your house."

Deni's heart thumped so loudly she was sure he could hear it. "OK," she said as casually as she could. "It starts at eleven. I'll pack a lunch—"

"Let me pack it," he said. "I make a four-star chicken-salad sandwich."

Dazed, she gave him her address. She couldn't believe this was happening. "It's a yellow two-story house on the west side of the street," she said. "With a lone pin oak tree in the front yard."

"I'll be there about ten-thirty," he said, turning to leave. "And if the kid with braces—what's his name, Rick?—calls to ask you out," he added, winking at her, "tell him you're already busy."

Chapter Three

"I wish you could see all the teddy bears they had at the toy store, Gram. I don't know why, but I liked this little guy best. He has such funny, close-set eyes," Deni said. She handed her grandmother a small teddy bear with a big blue ribbon around its neck. "I named him Henry. I'm taking him over to Chuck's this weekend. Think the baby will like him?"

"How could any child resist Henry's obvious charm?" her grandmother said. She smiled as she touched the bear's fur. "He's almost as soft as Belzy."

At the mention of her name, the old gray cat, curled up on one of the porch chairs, opened her eyes and lifted her head. Deni picked her up and began to stroke her. Belzy was without a doubt one of the largest, laziest cats on the face of the earth—and one of the prettiest. She was a companionable creature who liked to be around people and considered Deni's grandmother's old house her personal domain.

Deni sipped her lemonade. She and her grandmother were sitting on the big shady front porch, enjoying the sunny June afternoon. The soft breeze that rippled through the old wicker furniture set the wind chimes swaying, filling the air with their low, tinkling sounds. Deni's grandmother leaned against the thick pillows of an oversize wicker rocker, her legs resting on an old wicker stool, a lightweight quilt across her lap. Next to the rocker was a workbasket stuffed with a variety of projects. She was always doing something, whether she was reading or working on needlepoint. She always joked that having to rest so much was giving her a chance to catch up on things she had been meaning to do for forty years.

"Henry will look wonderful in the nursery. He'll be a loving reminder of you," her grandmother continued. She looked at Deni, her eyes twinkling. "Why, if I may ask, are you in such fine spirits this afternoon, my dear Denise? Unless I'm wrong, something more special than finding the perfect teddy bear has happened."

Deni grinned. "Can't hide anything from you, can I?" Just thinking about Mike made her so happy. She had wanted to tell her grandmother about him ever since she had arrived at the house an hour before. "Remember the guy I was telling you about? He works at the station?"

"Oh, yes. Let me see. I believe his name is—Mike?"

"Right," Deni answered.

"Well?" her grandmother prodded, a look of expectancy on her face, her faded blue eyes dancing.

"We're going to the lake tomorrow for the sailing regatta. Isn't that great? I can hardly believe it!"

"That's wonderful." Her grandmother smiled, then added, "I hope I meet this young man sometime."

"You'll like him, Gram," Deni said, beaming. "He's one of the interns at the station, and he's going to go to K.U. in the fall and—" She paused. "Are you feeling OK, Gram? You look pale."

"Just tired. I didn't sleep very well last night, but of course I'm much better than a week ago when this old heart of mine gave us all such a scare." She patted her chest. "I'm doing exactly what Dr. Brock told me to do—I rest two hours every morning, and rest or nap all afternoon, and I take my medicine faithfully." She reached into the workbasket and pulled out a package of old letters tied with a lace ribbon. "I was cleaning out a bureau drawer and came across these. Some of them are forty years old. Last night I started reading them, and then when I tried to sleep, I was too caught up in memories. But I think I'll rest fine tonight."

Deni took the packet from her grandmother's lap. It had a musty smell. Most of the letters were yellowed with age.

"I don't even know who all of them are from or why I saved them," her grandmother said. "They just struck me at the time as important, and I put them away. Would you read one to me, Deni? My eyes aren't as good as they used to be. I don't care which one—just pick one randomly."

Deni pulled a letter from the stack and studied the return address. "It's from Hazel Whitten—Great-Aunt Hazel!" she exclaimed.

"My sister," her grandmother murmured, closing her eyes. She had a happy look on her face. "Wonderful, sweet Hazel. We were always so close."

"I remember her, Gram. When I was little she came to visit you, and she brought me candy. I still remember it. It was blue, and I was afraid it was poison. But I ate it anyway, and it was delicious." Deni laughed. She settled herself on the wide porch railing, her back against the corner post, her feet stretched out in front of her. "OK, here goes. The date is February 3, 1937." She cleared her throat. " 'My Dear Lily, Robert and I have just returned from our trip to Germany. What we have been reading about the rise of this man Hitler and the power he has over the German people is all true.' Wow!" Deni said. "This is like a history lesson, Gram."

She continued the letter, reading her great-aunt Hazel's observations of the German people, their daily lives, and their politics. Deni was entranced. Reading about it in a letter was far different from reading it in her American history book. No wonder her grandmother had saved that letter.

When Deni had finished, her grandmother told her that, as teenagers, she and Hazel had both liked the young man who was courting their oldest sister, Emily. "I'm afraid we both made fools of ourselves more than once," she added and chuckled. "I don't know how Emily tolerated us. That young man ended up breaking her heart—or at least it was broken until she met Frank, the man she married." She paused. "Can't believe they're gone now," she said wistfully.

Deni pulled another letter from the stack, anxious to find a cheerful memory for her grandmother. She studied the envelope. "Hey! This one is from my father!" she said in astonishment. "It's addressed to you and Grandfather at the cabin in Maine."

"I'd forgotten that he wrote us once. What's the date?" her grandmother asked. She had already closed her eyes again, ready to listen.

"It's August 2, 1966, that's three years before I was born!" Deni carefully opened the envelope and pulled out the letter. She studied the handwriting, a large, expressive scrawl. She had never thought of her father as a letter writer. Whenever he came to mind, the first thing she recalled was his eyes, wrinkled at the corners when he smiled. She began to read the letter out loud.

" 'Dear Mother and Father.' He called you 'Mother' just like my mom does?"

"From the day he and your mother were married until his death," her grandmother answered. "He never felt awkward about it as some men do. I've known men who called their mothers-in-law Mrs.-So-and-So for fifty years. Not your father."

" 'Dear Mother and Father,' " Deni read. " 'I'm afraid I have some bad news to share. Since I'm writing this letter instead of Claire, you have already guessed that something has kept her from doing it herself.' " Deni glanced at her grandmother to see if she should continue reading. What if the letter brought up bad memories that disturbed her? But her grandmother's eyes were still closed, and she was slowly shaking her head in agreement as though she remembered very clearly what was about to be revealed. " 'Don't be concerned—she's going to be all right,' " Deni read. " 'I must tell you immediately that she suffered another miscarriage. This is especially hard for us both, for it's now eight years since we've been trying to have another child—since Chuckie was born.' " Deni was surprised. She had never heard her brother referred to as "Chuckie" before. It would have been funnier to her if the tone of the letter weren't so serious.

" 'The doctor has told us not to try again,' " she continued reading. " 'He says Claire's blood pressure is too high and that it's too dangerous to consider. We both regret this deeply, but three miscarriages have been terribly hard on Claire, and we must get on with our lives. We have decided to adopt a baby.' That's me!" Deni said, surprised. "He's talking about me!" Hastily she read on. This definitely was a treasure hunt, and the treasure was additional information about her own past.

" 'Yesterday we talked to an adoption agency. Since we're both in our midthirties, they tell us to be patient. We will not be given priority, and it may take some time before we reach the top of their list, especially since we're requesting a healthy infant girl. We hope you will share our conviction that we have made the right decision. We have enjoyed your letters and postcards. It sounds as though the coast is truly beautiful this year. With love, John.' "

Feeling confused, Deni looked up from the letter. She had never known about the miscarriages. Her mother had said they couldn't have more children after Chuck and had decided to adopt. That was all. She was always reluctant to talk about her own life and Deni's adoption.

Her father's writing style interested her. He sounded very proper and formal—almost out of another era. She couldn't remember if he had talked that way or not. *Probably not*, she decided. People had been taught to write that way then.

Deni's grandmother's eyes remained closed, her chair rocking back and forth, the smile still on her face. "It's so strange to be reading something my father wrote, Gram. I never knew him very well," Deni said softly. Tears filled her eyes. "I knew him as my daddy, but not—you know—as a person."

"Letters can be very revealing," her grandmother replied. "You can tell in that one how much your father cared for your mother. He was a wonderful man. By knowing him as a father you *did* know him as a person. He was one of those people who are the same whatever they do." She opened her eyes. "Your mother and I both had good husbands. And we both lost them when they were young. We have something else in common, too," she said gently, looking at Deni.

"What's that?"

"Wonderful daughters. I've always thought your mother was about as fine a daughter as anyone could have, and you're just as dear to her. We've both been fortunate."

"Gram—" Deni said and hesitated. She hadn't brought up the topic of her adoption to her grandmother in several years, but her father's letter seemed like a good lead-in to the subject. Her adoption wasn't something that Deni's grandmother talked about any more easily than her mother did. Still, her grandmother didn't seem threatened by the topic now, and Deni wanted desperately to discuss it.

Deni reached over and squeezed her grandmother's hand affectionately. "How come my mom won't talk to me about my adoption?"

she asked slowly. "Whenever I bring up the subject, this curtain drops between us. Is she afraid of something?"

"What do you mean?" her grandmother asked, surprised.

"Is she afraid that if I learn more about my birth parents I'll find out something terrible, something I can't handle? Like maybe that my birth mother was raped or that my birth father was a murderer or something?" Deni looked at her grandmother intently. "All I have to do is say the word 'adoption' and she gets this—this *look* on her face, and she sort of stiffens up. She always *says* she'll talk to me about anything, but she can't seem to discuss adoption. Sometimes I get this feeling that there's a terrible secret in my past that Mom either knows or suspects, and she just pretends I'm not adopted."

"Deni, do you ever question that she loves you?" her grandmother asked quietly.

"No, of course not, but—"

"Then why bring it up?" she asked gently. "She's told you what she knows. All of your legal records will be available to you when you're eighteen."

"That's not what I mean, Gram. *Why* is it so hard for her to talk about it with me? In the books she gave me on adoption when I was a kid, the parents always sat down and talked with their children about adoption. But Mom just gave me the books and told me to read them. She never talked to me about them. What's the big deal?"

Deni's grandmother looked thoughtful. "There are no secrets that I am aware of, no awful truths to be uncovered. You do have a point about your mother's attitude, Deni, but I don't think you're going to be able to change her. Instead you must try to understand her—and perhaps I can help." She paused, weighing her words as she rearranged the quilt on her lap. Deni waited silently, staring out at the long, shady lawn with the large trees she had loved to climb when she was little.

"I think your mother very easily forgets that you are adopted," her grandmother began. "She thinks of you as her own flesh and blood. As you just learned from your father's letter, she couldn't have more children after Chuck. That was very sad for her. But from the day she and your father adopted you, she loved you as her own. So when the subject comes up—"

"It reminds her that I'm not," Deni finished. "I *do* understand that, Gram. But if we could just be open about it . . ." She trailed off.

"Well, you know in my day, when children were adopted as infants, they weren't even told they were adopted. For your mother to be honest with you wasn't easy for her. I think she would have gladly kept you from knowing."

"Don't you think my brown eyes and hair might have made other people—and me—a little suspicious?"

"Not necessarily," her grandmother answered. "We have brown-eyed and brown-haired people in our family tree. We could have come up with enough examples for you."

Deni looked down at the letter in her hand from her father. "Sometimes I feel like such an imposter. I have you and Mom and Chuck, but I'm not really related to you. Somewhere there are people who *are* my blood family, and I wonder what I would be like if I lived with them. How would I be different than I am now? Do you understand, Gram?"

Her grandmother looked at her sympathetically. "I do, Deni. I'm sure your curiosity is perfectly natural. I don't see how it could be otherwise. I wish I could say something more that would give you comfort."

Deni gave her grandmother a quick smile. "I know it's not easy for you to talk about, either. Thanks for what you've told me, Gram." She studied her father's handwriting. "Do you think—"

"What, dear?" Her grandmother sounded tired.

"Do you think my mom will ever remarry? She's not *that* old yet," Deni said.

Her grandmother chuckled. "I doubt it," she answered. "She loved your father very much. I don't think another man could ever measure up to him in her eyes."

"I guess you're right," Deni agreed. "I sure miss him." She looked out at the lawn. Memories flooded over her, bits and pieces of moments: her father tucking her into bed at night, her father playing softball with her,

39

her father pointing to sights outside the window on their train trip to Chicago many years before. And then, on that fateful day six years before, her mother told her that her father wouldn't be coming home again. She remembered the words "automobile accident" and something about a truck crossing the center line, a head-on collision, instant death.

Abruptly Deni shut off those thoughts. It was too painful to think about her father.

She smiled weakly at her grandmother. "I'm going to do some work on the flower beds, Gram. I brought my swimsuit with me. I'll work over in this section of the yard so we can visit while you rest."

Deni stopped in the kitchen, found an apple in the refrigerator, and perched on the stool next to the stove to eat it. She loved her grandmother's kitchen. Large windows had been added ten years before, and tall trees kept the room shady all day. Deni sat there recalling informal meals at the kitchen table; sitting at that table, they had watched the seasons change in the backyard.

Still munching her apple, Deni went into the dining room. On top of a curio cabinet in one corner were small cameo-framed pictures of her grandmother's parents when they were newlyweds. Her grandmother's father had a severe expression on his face and wore a starched white collar. Her grandmother's mother looked plump and kind and very, very young. They had come to Kansas from England so he could work for a cousin who owned a successful lumberyard. Deni had heard many stories from her grandmother about growing up living over a local hardware store.

When Deni was a little younger, she had loved being alone in that old house. She would pretend that she was a celebrity and was giving a tour to Barbara Walters and her television audience of millions. She would explain aloud where each picture on the wall, each vase, or each figurine had come from and why they were special. Barbara was always enchanted with her, of course.

The house was such a contrast to Deni's own. Three years before she and her mother had moved out of an older house to their new house near the lake. Chuck had married Kara, and Deni's mother had decided that since there would be just the two of them, they would be more comfortable in a new, smaller house. Deni had always suspected that her mother just didn't want to stay any longer in the house she had shared with her husband because the memories were too painful.

But the newer home was so ordinary compared to their other house. It was in sharp contrast to her grandmother's little Victorian house with its gingerbread trim, big yard, and huge old trees that shaded the house all summer, keeping it cool.

Deni's mother had picked a small, yellow two-story house in a new part of town. The streets were wide and the trees were young offering little shade. Even though the design of each house was supposed to be different, the houses all looked and felt the same to Deni. The lots were uniform in size, and every house had a double-wide driveway, the same sidewalk, and the same green patch of lawn. There just wasn't anything interesting about their house. But Deni did know that it was easy for her mother to care for. Her grandmother was constantly having something repaired, yet she refused to give up her house and move in with her daughter and granddaughter. She considered the inconvenience of keeping up the house a small price to pay for staying in the place she loved most.

She wouldn't allow anyone to live with her. Deni's mother had told her many times that they would move in with her if she wanted them to. But Deni's grandmother had claimed that she needed her independence.

Deni picked up the eight-by-ten picture of herself, Chuck, and their parents that usually sat on the end table by the sofa in the living room. It was the last picture taken of the four of them. She was ten at the time, and Chuck was twenty. Everybody looked very happy. Deni could still remember the day it was taken. Her father had made a festive occasion of going to the photographer's studio and had treated them all to ice cream afterward.

Abruptly Deni set the picture down. She simply couldn't think about her father right then. She missed him too much.

Deni wondered what it was that she needed

from her family. Her father had been a wonderful man. She and her mother were very close: Chuck was right, they *were* like best friends. And yet, somewhere, there were those two other people, a man and a woman, who were her real mother and father. What were they like? Was there some deep dark secret about them? Sometimes her curiosity tormented her. She wanted to know everything.

What she had told Chuck that morning was true: She grew up dreaming a whole fantasy in which her natural family—if she could find them—would welcome her with open arms. Somehow her mother must know this and was afraid of losing her to this other family.

Deni wandered into the bathroom and changed into her swimsuit. She twirled around in front of the full-length mirror. All that indoor tennis and volleyball had paid off during the winter months. She looked fit and trim—and pale. It was time to get outside into the sunshine!

The sidewalk leading to the garage behind the house was cool on her bare feet, and a light breeze stirred the trees. Kansas would get much hotter before the summer was over. In fact, by August, everyone would be desperate for a day as pleasant as that one. That day, for the sake of her suntan, she wished the temperature were twenty degrees warmer.

She found an empty trash can and carried it to the daisy bed on the south side of the house and began to weed the plants. The warm sun felt good on her back and shoulders.

Deni thought about Mike while she worked. It was always scary to go out with someone for the first time. She had never gone out with anyone she was so attracted to. But even though she was shy and tongue-tied around him, she felt as though she had known him for a long time. Even her grandmother could tell, just from the way Deni talked, that Mike was different from her past boyfriends.

The year before she had dated two boys, one her age and one a year older. She didn't like either one of them anymore. She had gone to the prom with a boy named Randy. They had double-dated with Lori and the guy she was dating then, one of Randy's friends. He had called her only once after the prom. She had told him, as gently as she could, that she didn't want to go out again. He didn't call again.

Deni smiled as she thought of her conversation with Mike that morning. She still couldn't believe how it worked out. She got shivers just thinking about her own aggressiveness. She had asked him out—and it had worked! She wondered, though, if he had come to the lobby to find her. Maybe he had been planning to ask her out!

Deni wished she knew more about him. She was still certain she had seen him somewhere with someone she knew, and it bothered her. She pictured a beautiful blond with him. But who? And where had she seen him?

She finished weeding the daisy bed and got her sketchbook, then sat down on the lawn, the sun on her shoulders, and began to draw, deftly outlining the flowers with the house behind them. The very first sketch pleased her, and she filled in the details. If her grandmother was still napping when she left for home later, she would leave it, along with a little note saying, "Lots of love, Deni," on the table next to her so she would find it when she woke up. She smiled at the thought; she knew the sketch would make her grandmother happy.

Chapter Four

When Deni awoke Saturday morning, her room was gray. *Oh, no!* she thought. *Not today.*

No light was peeking through the blinds, which meant it was overcast—maybe even raining. The regatta would be cancelled, and Deni would have to face another dreary, dull weekend. And since she couldn't very well ask Mike out again, she would have to wait for him to reschedule their outing.

Deni wanted to go back to sleep and just forget about her disappointment. But she knew she was wide awake. She turned on her bedside lamp and reached for a book to read. She glanced at the clock. It was only a little after five! No wonder her room was gray. Anxiously she opened her blinds and looked at the eastern sky. It was awash with the first glimmers of morning light, pinks and blues that promised a beautiful, clear day.

47

Deni collapsed back into her pillows and laughed at her own silliness. Then she tried to decide what to do. Mike wasn't coming until ten-thirty. How was she going to keep herself busy until then?

Tugging off her nightgown, Deni tried on the outfit she had laid out the night before. She considered several other combinations of shorts and tops, but finally settled on the first one—white shorts and a new aqua blue polo shirt. She had bought it the night before after visiting her grandmother. *If only my legs were more tan,* Deni thought. But the weather had been too rainy lately for that.

By eight o'clock Deni had cleaned her room, taken her bath, washed and fixed her hair, and gotten dressed. She opened her new *Seventeen* magazine, but couldn't concentrate on it. She pulled out a piece of paper to try to write Lori, but she couldn't keep her mind on that, either. After repeatedly catching herself doodling the name "Mike" all over the stationery, Deni decided to write to Lori the next day—*after* the regatta. She would have more to tell her then.

Sam was scratching at the front door as Deni wandered downstairs, so she let him in. She could hear her mother in the kitchen making coffee. If she went back to her room and stayed there until Mike arrived, she wouldn't have to face breakfast.

"Deni?" Mrs. Lambert called.

"It's me," Deni said, walking reluctantly into the kitchen. She sat down at the table. "Please don't talk about food, Mother," Deni added. "I can't take it."

"I've never seen you act this jumpy before a date," her mother commented, setting a glass of orange juice in front of Deni. "Not even when you were going to the prom with Randy. What's the difference this time?"

"Nothing, Mom," Deni said, avoiding her eyes. "Well, maybe Mike's a *little* different," she admitted. "He's—well, he's—" She was at a loss for words. "I don't know what it is. I hardly know him. I can just tell he's different, that's all." She drank the orange juice in one gulp.

Mrs. Lambert smiled understandingly. When Deni got up to wash her glass, she waved her away. "I'm afraid our china would never be the same if I let you do the dishes this morning. Why don't you check your bike tires to make sure they're ready for today's ride?"

"I forgot all about that!" Deni cried. "What if one of my tires is flat?" She ran to the garage and got her bike out, breathing a sigh of relief as she saw that everything was in good condition. She stuck her head back in the kitchen door. "I'll ride it down to the station on the corner and get some air in the tires, just to be sure," she called to her mother. "Maybe by the time I get back, he'll be here."

Deni was back by ten, her bike ready for the ride. She spent the next half hour brushing her hair, pulling it back with a ribbon first and then snatching the ribbon off. She finally gathered it up on the back of her head, catching it in a wide barrette so it wouldn't blow around on the bike ride. She tucked her sketch pad and drawing pencils into her backpack and slung the pack over one shoulder. Then she sat down on her bed. There simply was nothing else to do.

At ten-thirty Deni heard a car pull up in front of their house. She glanced out her bedroom window and saw Mike getting out of a small blue Honda Civic. His bike was perched on top in a bike rack, and after he got it down, he leaned it against the tree in the front yard. A moment later the door bell rang. She panicked. What was she going to say to him? What could they possibly talk about all afternoon?

She held her breath as her mother answered the door and invited him in. Deni wasn't sure whether or not to wait for her mother to call her. She glanced frequently in the mirror. Maybe she should change her clothes—no, she looked fine. Her hair looked shiny and casual. Her eyes were dark and luminous, and her cheeks were flushed with excitement.

Deni strained to hear the conversation between her mother and Mike. Her mother was laughing. She decided to go downstairs and join them. That would be better than waiting. She slowly descended the stairs, taking deep breaths as she went. A moment later she was in the living room.

"Hi, Mike," Deni said. She hoped she sounded more at ease than she felt.

He waved at her and nodded, then turned back to Deni's mother, who was talking about work. Deni could hardly believe that Mike was actually there in her own house. He didn't look the least bit out of place; in fact, he seemed as relaxed and comfortable as if he came there all the time. He was wearing cotton shorts and a knit shirt. It was the first time she had seen him in anything but jeans and a T-shirt.

Deni had been worried that they would stand around in awkward silence for a few minutes. Instead, Mike and her mother were deep in conversation, and she couldn't get a word in edgewise. Deni decided to stand back and listen.

"Then it must be your aunt who is one of the publication editors at the Menninger Foundation," Mrs. Lambert said. She sounded pleased. "I've known Eleanor for years. She's very highly thought of by everyone there." Mike and Deni's mother traded notes on all the people they both knew who worked at the foundation.

Finally Deni cleared her throat and, looking pointedly at her watch, said, "Uh, Mike, we don't want to miss the beginning of the regatta."

"No, sorry. I didn't know it was getting so late," Mike said. He picked up his backpack by the front door, and Mrs. Lambert stood on the porch and waved as they got on their bikes.

As they rode down the driveway together,

Deni felt so happy she could have burst. The weather couldn't have been more perfect—sunny and warm and a vivid sky scattered with a few billowy clouds. And Mike—*Mike!*—was with her, and they would spend the next several hours together.

They pedaled along side by side on the paved road, pointing out to each other the patches of blooming wild flowers that edged the green, rolling meadows and fields of young corn they passed. To Deni everything seemed so alive. Birds sang energetically, and a herd of cattle that clustered against a fence gazed soulfully at them as they passed by.

Deni realized she had never seen Mike outside before. Somehow he seemed even more at home riding a bicycle than he did in the television studio or in her living room. Or was it just that Mike fit in well anywhere? She glanced at him out of the corner of her eye. It would be so easy to fall in love with him—he was so handsome! He had been so polite to her mother, Deni thought, yet it seemed to come naturally to him; it wasn't as if he were out to impress her. Deni realized that she wanted her mother to like Mike. That thought stopped her. Why? Because she liked Mike more than she had ever liked any boy? She shook her head and put on an extra burst of speed as the lake came into view.

Sailboats of all sizes gently skimmed the glassy waters of Lake Shawnee, their colorful sails billowing in the soft breeze of the warm day. Deni and Mike walked their bikes to a spot on a low hill where they could watch the boats and also see the gazebo on one of the points overlooking the lake. Nearby, two dogs chased each other, and a little boy and his father played with a small motorized airplane. Groups of picnickers were everywhere, drawn to the lake by the regatta and the beauty of the day.

They spread out the lightweight blanket Mike had brought, then unpacked and ate the lunch he had made, feasting on chicken salad sandwiches, potato chips, apples, and fresh brownies. Deni was surprised to find she was hungry and that her stomach was calm enough that she could eat. Neither of them spoke as they ate. Deni didn't feel like making conversation, and Mike seemed content to sit next to her in companionable silence.

Deni wadded up the last piece of waxed paper and tucked it away in her backpack. "I'm stuffed," she proclaimed, leaning back on her elbows. "You really do make four-star chicken salad."

"Thank you," Mike said. "My mother wants all of her kids to have at least some basic survival skills. So she has made sure we can all cook a couple of things."

"I could definitely survive on that lunch," Deni said. She glanced over at Mike. He was looking out at the boats that were drifting along in front of them. A breeze was ruffling his hair, and he seemed relaxed. Deni felt comfortable and happy. Usually eating in front of a boy made Deni self-conscious, but she hadn't even thought about it.

Deni took her sketchbook out of her backpack and quickly drew one of the sailboats. It was a rough sketch, hardly more than a vague shape. But she liked to begin simply, until she drew something she really wanted to spend time on.

Mike peered over her shoulder. She forced herself to concentrate on her sketch.

"You make that look easy," Mike said. "I can't do it at all. Maybe that's why I take pictures."

"How long have you been interested in photography?" Deni asked, her eyes still focused on the sailboat she was copying.

"Seven or eight years," Mike said. "I went through a stack of old *Life* magazines when I was about nine. I couldn't get over the photographs. I spent hours looking at them. Finally my mother gave me a simple camera, thinking I would get it out of my system.

"But I was immediately hooked," he recalled. "In fact, I got my first summer job when I was thirteen taking care of our neighbor's yard just so I could buy a better camera and film. How about you? When did you start to draw?"

She gazed out over the lake, trying to remember. "I don't know," she finally said. "I've just always done it. If I don't have paper, then I doodle on the corners of newspapers or something. I probably started with crayons on my bedroom wall," she giggled. "Mom has some stories about my 'early' art."

It was almost one o'clock. The day was slipping by quickly. Mike loaded his 35-mm camera and then left Deni to take pictures of the little boy with the airplane.

A shiver passed over her. He wasn't as tall as her brother, but he was considerably taller than her own five-four. She liked his slender body and the quick way he moved.

Deni had never been attracted to boys who spent all their time on body building and athletics and trying to prove how macho they were. The school jocks had never interested her unless they went out for baseball, the one sport she enjoyed watching. Lori had dragged her to almost all the football and basketball games in the past two years at high school. Lori had had crushes on every player, but Deni had remained aloof.

Mike walked back up the hill and flopped down on his stomach. "I think I got a couple of good pictures. I wish we were out on the water sailing. I go out to my cousins' house in the country to sail whenever I can. Their house is on a small lake."

Deni watched the boats. "I'd love to try sailing," she said.

"I want to have my own boat someday," he said. "Right now it's all I can do to support my car and my camera and still put some money aside for college." He turned over on his back and closed his eyes.

Deni worked on a troublesome sail on her

sketch. She wanted to ask him if he was dating someone. She felt more certain than ever that she had seen Mike with a blond girl and that she was much more than a good friend. But how could she ask? She couldn't just say, "Why do I keep having this vision of you with a sexy blond?" She had to be more subtle than that! Maybe she could lead into the question. "Do you have brothers and sisters?" Deni asked.

"Two brothers," he replied. "Do you have anyone besides Chuck?"

"Nope," she answered. "What are your brothers like?"

He frowned and scratched his head. "Well, let's see. They're both older than I am, and they were both good athletes in school. Their names are Bob and Eliot. Bob played basketball, and Eliot was on the football team."

That wasn't going to lead to a discussion about a girlfriend. How could she work around to that? She concentrated on her sketch. "Did you play sports in school?"

"I was on the swim team my sophomore year but decided to spend my time with the school newspaper instead of sports. I played on the intramural teams when I could."

"What do your brothers do now?" Deni asked. She hoped she didn't sound as though she were interviewing him.

Mike sat up and picked up his camera. He focused it on her and fiddled with the adjustments. She made a funny face at him as he snapped a picture. "Eliot is a schoolteacher in Wichita, and Bob is starting law school at the University of Kansas this fall. It'll be fun with both of us living in Lawrence. He seems very intent on being a lawyer—the family's first."

"Do you have a major picked out?"

He lay down on his stomach again and propped himself on one arm, watching her draw. "That's a tough one," he said thoughtfully. "I love photography, but it's a hard field to make a living in. Of course my dad thinks I should major in business, like everyone else these days, but I just don't have the interest. When you take a good picture and you're in the lab and watch it develop, it's just the greatest feeling there is."

Deni nodded. "I'm that way about art. A lot of times I'm just sketching to be doing something. But when I get going on an idea I like, I could draw forever. I've been sketching my grandmother's house and flower gardens for her. Sort of a series."

"You're really good," Mike commented.

"Thanks. I'd like to see some of your photos," Deni answered.

"But as for what I want to major in, well, I just hope I can decide soon and not waste a lot of time in college trying to get it figured out. I might major in radio-television production," Mike said. "I applied for the internship at the station this summer so I could see how I liked it. A lot of the work is routine, but then again I get some real interesting assignments. I had a great time filming this little kid a few days ago."

"Do you mean Freddie?"

Mike nodded.

"Chuck told me about him. He figured I'd be interested in the series since I'm adopted," Deni said.

"You are?"

"Haven't you noticed how different Chuck and I look?" she asked casually. She wished she hadn't brought up the subject. Now he would have questions.

He shrugged. "I didn't think anything about it. Bob has reddish-blond hair, Eliot has black hair, and mine's brown. But," Mike added, laughing, "we all have identical Irish faces—or so my great-aunt Gladys says. You're adopted? That really surprises me. You seem so—"

"Normal?" she wanted to kick herself for opening herself up to this. "I remember when my best friend, Lori, found out I was adopted. We were in seventh grade. For weeks she treated me like I had some strange disease. I finally told her to cut it out."

"I didn't mean to make it sound like that," Mike said, instantly apologetic. "It must be something you're comfortable about, or you wouldn't have told me."

"Most of the time I am," Deni said.

"What's it like?"

"What?"

"Does it feel different—you know what I mean—does it feel—well, how does it feel not to be related—biologically related—to your family?" Mike asked.

Deni was on her guard. How could she explain something like that? "I was adopted when I was three days old," she said cautiously. "I don't know anything else."

"But what's it like?" Mike repeated.

Deni looked at him. His eyes were kind, inquisitive, trusting. Still, he was asking her something so personal that she didn't know if she could reply. No one had ever asked her that question before—not Lori, and certainly no one in her family.

She hesitated, feeling a little awkward and suddenly shy. "I'm not sure I can tell you so you'd understand," she said at last. "I'm afraid you'll get the idea that I'm not grateful to have been adopted or that I don't love my family. I do, really. It's just that—"

Mike waited patiently while Deni searched for the words. She swallowed hard, her words coming slowly at first. "It's like never being completely connected to the people you love best," she said hesitantly. "Sometimes I'm so curious about my natural parents I can hardly stand it. Who do I look like? What's in me? What abilities, what talents, what defects? Sometimes it hurts. I wonder exactly why I was given up. Sometimes I get scared. I worry that maybe I'll get sick, and it'll turn out to be some weird genetic disease—something hereditary and it's a life or death matter that I have a blood transfusion from an immediate member of my biological family.

Things like that," Deni finished, suddenly embarrassed.

She looked out over the lake. A bird gracefully skimmed the water's edge, adding to the picture-perfect scene. How could she explain her need? It was like an itch that wouldn't go away. It was *there*, and it was troublesome. No one knew about it except her, and no doctor could cure it.

"It seems strange we would be talking about this. Just yesterday morning Chuck asked me about it, and then I read a letter at my grandmother's that my father wrote before I was born saying he and my mom were going to try to adopt. That's a lot of coincidences," she said. She wrinkled her nose at him, her mood suddenly light. "Why are *you* so curious?"

Mike looked puzzled. "I don't know. It's just sort of fascinating. Even when I'm not taking pictures, I watch people. I always try to guess whether they're related. Usually I can tell because of a family resemblance or because they act alike, and I just figured you and Chuck were brother and sister. Maybe you don't think you look all that much like each other, but you're a lot alike."

"We are? I've never thought so," Deni said.

"You are, really. You're both serious and funny and nice."

She put her sketch pad down and flopped over on her stomach next to him. She felt very calm as she turned and looked intently at him. "And you're very full of questions, and I have no idea when you've had the time to make all these observations since we've practically just met," she said.

"Photographers are inquisitive by nature," he said, looking steadily into her eyes. "As to when I made these observations, well, let's just say I form my opinions quickly."

Mike was so close to her that Deni could smell his after-shave and the clean scent of his shirt. She wanted him to kiss her. She wanted that very much. She smiled at him, amazed by her own calm. She was ready. It was the first time she had ever truly wanted a boy to kiss her.

Mike simply stared at her for a moment and then turned away, a shadow crossing his face.

"Come on!" he said. Abruptly he got to his feet and put his camera around his neck. "Let's walk down to the water. I'll ask the people behind us to watch our stuff." She felt stunned. What had she done wrong? Had she been too forward?

Deni stood up while Mike went over to some nearby picnickers. When he returned, they began to walk in silence down the hill.

It was so confusing to Deni. What had happened? She had wanted him to kiss her. Why hadn't he?

"Mike—" she began.

"Yeah?" he answered, his voice pleasant and detached. They walked along the water's edge. Out on the lake, the boats continued to float on the breeze.

What could she say? Deni couldn't just ask why he hadn't kissed her. She was sure it had something to do with another girl. "Would you like to come over tonight and watch television?" she asked impulsively. There, she had done it again, making all the advances. She had to stop that.

"I can't. Maybe another time," Mike said shortly.

There was someone else. Now she was sure. Deni was just a Saturday diversion. Just a friend to go to the lake with. He had a date with the blond that night.

By the time they watched the boats awhile, walked back to their spot, and packed everything up, it was four o'clock. Mike set a fast pace for the ride home, but Deni had no problem keeping up with him. Winded from the bike ride, they paused in her driveway, breathing hard.

"That was fun, Deni," Mike said, grinning. "Let me see the sketch when you finish."

She smiled back at him. "Sure you don't have time to come in for some lemonade?"

"Can't today. Sorry. I have some errands to do for my mother. I'll take a raincheck, though."

Deni nodded in agreement. Their eyes met for a moment. Then Mike put his bike on the car rack and got into the front seat.

Deni watched him drive away. For several minutes she didn't move. Finally she put her bike in the garage and walked slowly into the house.

"Hi, honey," her mother said.

"Hi, Mom." She set her backpack on the kitchen table, avoiding her mother's eyes. She knew she had been watching out the window.

"I was hoping you'd bring him in," Mrs. Lambert commented.

"Sorry, he had to get home. We were running late."

"Did you have a good time?" she asked Deni. She sounded anxious.

Deni hesitated. "I don't know, Mom. I guess I did, but—"

"But what?"

"I just don't understand guys," Deni said, her voice full of frustration. "Mike seems so nice, but he was secretive about something. I think he has a girlfriend." She sat down at the kitchen table and sipped the lemonade her mother put in front of her. She knew there would be more questions. Mrs. Lambert and Deni always chatted after one of them had been away.

Mrs. Lambert poured a cup of coffee and sat down across the table from her. They smiled at each other, and Deni started to talk about her date.

Chapter Five

Right after dinner on Saturday night, Deni tried to put all thoughts of Mike aside and pay her brother a visit. She had Henry the Bear tucked under one arm as she rang the doorbell at Chuck and Kara's home.

When Kara opened the door, Deni noticed how pale and tired she looked. Still, her face lit up when Deni handed her the teddy bear.

"Chuck's not here," Kara said, inviting her in. "He went to the hardware store. You know how trips like that go—it may take him awhile to get back. I know I look awful. I think I must have a little touch of the flu or something." She poured Deni a glass of iced tea in the kitchen, then walked down the hallway toward the nursery. "I thought the last couple of months were supposed to be pretty easy," she remarked.

"Are you going to be able to keep working?" Deni asked.

Kara ran her hand through her short, light brown hair. "I want to. We need my salary since I'm taking off six months after the baby is born. I was planning to work right up until I went into the hospital."

"Maybe you should just rest—" Deni began.

"I'll feel better tomorrow," Kara said, trying to sound convincing. "I finished the curtains for the nursery. Come look."

"Oh, Kara, the whole room is perfect!" Deni exclaimed, as they entered the room. "I can't believe it! Last week it was your sewing room, and now it's just begging for a baby to move in. I love it!"

Kara looked around the small room proudly. Teddy bears lined a shelf above the new white chest of drawers and changing table. Airy white curtains trimmed with colorful ribbon hung at the window. The new wallpaper, with its pattern of teddy bears, now covered two walls. Kara placed Henry the Bear in the crib on top of the soft lambswool covering, propping him up against a tiny baby pillow.

Her eyes glowed with pleasure. "He's wonderful, Deni. The final, perfect touch. Like you said, all we need now is the baby." Kara hugged her. "Wait till Chuck gets home and sees him. He loves all these teddy bears, and this one is the best yet."

Suddenly Kara moaned softly and clutched her side. "There's another one of those pains," she gasped, breathless for a moment.

Deni was alarmed. "You should rest. Can I

get you anything? Or do anything to help?" she asked.

"I'll just sit down a few minutes. So far I haven't had more than a couple in a row." She still sounded out of breath.

"Are they contractions?" Deni asked. "Isn't it too early for that?"

"They *are* contractions," Kara explained, "but 'false' ones. They're not uncommon, lots of women get them. They don't necessarily mean anything is wrong. I guess my body is warming up for the Big Event in two months," she added, smiling weakly.

They went into the living room and settled into the deep cushiony sofa. Kara awkwardly placed her feet on the coffee table. She stared at the flower arrangement that covered the fireplace opening in the summer, and a moment later a tear trickled down her cheek. Deni patted her hand, and Kara gave her a quick smile as she pulled a tissue from her pocket and wiped her eyes. "Sorry about that," she murmured. "It's just that those pains scare me. And I'm tired. Everything's been fine until the last few weeks, and I want so badly for the rest of the pregnancy to go well. This baby means everything to Chuck and me. It took me two years to get pregnant, and we couldn't stand it if something happened now."

"Nothing is going to happen," Deni said soothingly. "Your doctor says—"

"My doctor doesn't really know," Kara said quickly. "I talked to him this morning, and all he said was to take it real easy. But I'm worried. It's too early for the baby to be born."

Deni tried to think of something comforting to say. She hadn't known it had taken two years for Kara to get pregnant. Two years! She thought about her mother—she had tried for several years to have a baby and had finally had to adopt Deni.

"Maybe you should see your doctor again," she ventured.

Kara nodded in agreement. "I probably will in the next day or two." She tried to smile. "Sorry to act like this. Most of the time I'm fine. I just want this baby so badly. It isn't even born yet, and already I love it so much." She gently rubbed her stomach. "I'm sure all pregnant women are like this."

"Of course," Deni said. "Having a baby must be the most fantastic experience there is."

"It's pretty special," Kara said. "Sometimes I think I've been waiting all my life to become a parent. And Chuck, too. He's going to be the best father there ever was." She smiled and looked at Deni. "When I went to see Grandmother this afternoon she told me you had a very special date today. I've been waiting to hear about it."

Deni laughed self-consciously. "How many hours do you want to listen?" she asked, settling into the deep sofa pillows. They chatted until Chuck came in to join them.

"That's quite a letter, Gram," Deni said when she had finished reading several pages her grandfather had written in 1941. Her grandmother was resting in bed that day. It was raining outside—typical for a Monday—and she had complained of being more tired than usual. Deni knew she would sleep most of the afternoon.

The old woman's face glowed with pleasure. "When your grandfather wrote that, he had had to remain in Topeka to finish up some business while we went to Maine," she said. "Your mother must have been about seven then, and my brother Harold drove us all the way to Maine. We went to the beach every day, and Harold helped your mother make a shell necklace. I remember that so well!"

She stroked Belzy, who was curled up beside her on the bed. "It was such a hot summer in Kansas, but lovely on the East Coast. I hated leaving your grandfather here alone, but he insisted. He wasn't fond of writing letters, but he was very faithful about it."

Deni looked at the aged sheets of linen stationery in her hands. Her grandfather's writing was almost indecipherable. He had dutifully commented on the weather, the condition of the flower beds, and the latest decisions of the city council. There were no formal expressions of affection in the letter, yet as Deni read aloud, her grandmother seemed to have heard love in every line.

"Tell me again how you and Grandfather met," Deni said. "I haven't heard that story in a long time."

Her grandmother relaxed against her pillows. "In college. I was a new student, a freshman. My parents had sold some land they owned to pay for my tuition, and I was supposed to study home economics for at least two years. Then I would teach school. I went on a picnic with some girlfriends, and we were joined by a group of university men—your grandfather was one of them. We had a chaperon there, of course." She chuckled. "*Everything* was very well supervised in those days. Well, Theodore, your grandfather, and I just hit it off. After that I didn't have any interest in even talking to other young men. He was the only one for me."

"My first date with Mike was a picnic," Deni mused. "That's a coincidence!"

"But you haven't heard from him since then, have you?" her grandmother asked.

"No," Deni said, looking away, hoping the hurt didn't show on her face. "How did you know?"

"Yesterday you told me about your day at the lake with him on Saturday, but today you haven't mentioned him. All you've told me about is giving Kara the teddy bear Saturday night. And you seem restless. It's difficult waiting, isn't it? But he will call you."

"When?" Deni asked quickly. "Why didn't I hear from him yesterday? It was a Sunday—he must have been home. Boys! They can drive you so crazy! We really had a good time Saturday. Now it's Monday, and it's like he just dropped off the edge of the earth. I even tried to see him this morning at work, but when I went to the studio he wasn't around. I guess the camera crew was out on assignment."

Deni sighed and looked out the window at the light mist that had been falling since midmorning. She didn't want to tell her grandmother that she had been the one to suggest going to the lake in the first place or that Mike had treated her strictly as a friend. "Maybe he'll call me tonight," she said hopefully. "I'll probably spend all my time listening for the phone."

"Would it be completely inappropriate for you to call him?" her grandmother asked.

"I would, Gram, but I can't think of anything to say. I'd need a reason for calling," Deni answered.

"Would he?" her grandmother prodded her.

"Would he what?" Deni asked.

"I'm under the impression that you would be pleased to have him call just to chat. Why can't you do the same?"

"I—just can't. A girl can call a guy, but you can't be real obvious about it. Besides, I've already—I need a reason to call or else—"

"It looks like you're chasing him," her grandmother said, finishing the sentence.

"Right! How'd you know?" Deni asked.

Her grandmother smiled. "Some things never change. It's a wonderful new world for women out there, yet the etiquette of courtship is basically the same as it's always been. I don't remember how I got your grandfather to come visit me as often as I wanted him to, but sooner or later we worked it out."

Deni giggled. Then her grandmother began to laugh, and for a moment Deni felt that they shared a very special secret. Suddenly a branch outside rattled against the window, interrupting their laughter. Deni ran to the window. The wind had begun to blow, and it was getting darker. The rain was coming down harder, and lightning cut across the sky.

"Brrr! I should have brought my sweater," Deni said. "This is turning into a major summer storm. I'll go check to make sure all the windows in the other rooms are closed."

When she returned, she sat down in the bedside chair, watching through the window as the storm pounded the daisy bed. She turned and saw that her grandmother had fallen asleep, her mouth a perfect *O* as she snored softly.

Now what? Deni couldn't weed the flower beds in hard rain like that, and she didn't feel like reading a book or sketching. The house felt dark and cold. Wind rattled the windows, and thunder boomed overhead. She stared at the telephone. Waiting for Mike to get in touch with her was driving her crazy. Maybe he never would. Maybe he had had a rotten time and had only pretended he was enjoying himself. Deni was sure now that Mike had to have a girlfriend. If he thought that Deni was getting too interested in him, he would probably cut her off completely; he would be too nice to lead anyone on. Deni wondered what would happen if she ran into him at work. He would probably just ignore her.

If only Lori were home! Deni thought. Then they could talk about Mike and go shopping or to a movie. Deni could call her other friends, Jana or Kris, but she didn't feel like seeing either of them. She wasn't in the mood for shopping anyway. She had to save *some* of her paycheck.

Thunder boomed, and the rain poured down. Her grandmother slept on, undisturbed by the storm. Deni folded the letter from her grandfather and put it back into its envelope. Now, that might be a task for her. Maybe it would help if she put all of the old letters in order by the dates they were written. That way she could read them to her grandmother in order. The letters would become a real history of her grandmother's past that way.

Deni began to shift through the envelopes. She had learned to recognize handwriting. She could easily pick out that of her great-aunt's and her grandfather's, since so many of those had been saved.

Deni paused as she came to an envelope addressed to her grandmother in her mother's neat handwriting. The postmark said August 10, 1969. It took her a moment to realize why that date gnawed at her. Then she figured it out. It was dated two days after her birth.

For a moment her hand froze. Then, very slowly, she pulled a half-dozen sheets of thin, almost transparent, stationery from the envelope, the blue-ink words almost jumping out from the pages. She paused again. Something was holding her back. It was meant for her grandmother. Her grandfather had died in 1968. This letter wasn't meant for her. Then, very slowly, she read:

Dear Mother,

We have the most exciting news! Mrs. Blair at the adoption agency called us yesterday, and they have a baby girl for us! Our long wait is over!

The mother has already signed the papers, and we went to the hospital to see our new daughter last night. She's beautiful! She has lots of dark hair and lovely pink skin. She's just perfect in every way.

We will bring her home tomorrow. We can hardly believe it! Chuckie is very excited and is helping us give the nursery a fresh coat of paint.

We've decided to name her Denise. We think we will call her Dee Dee for short, but we're not sure yet.

Deni shuddered. At least "Dee Dee" hadn't stuck as a nickname. She was grateful for that. She anxiously read on.

We don't know much about the mother except that . . .

She quickly turned the page over, but what was on the back appeared to be the end of the letter. Her hands shaking, she tried to find the next sheet. Everything was out of order!

She glanced at her sleeping grandmother. Had she known this letter was in there? Probably she had forgotten it was in the stack. She might be upset—perhaps very upset—that Deni was reading it. With her heart condition, it was vitally important that nothing happened to upset her.

Deni knew she had to finish the letter quickly. She had to find the next sheet! What *did* they know about her mother?

It had gotten darker in the room, and Deni hurriedly reached to turn on the lamp by the chair, almost knocking it over. She fumbled with the thin sheets of stationery. Where *was* the next page! Quickly she put the pages in order, then went back and reread the line she had been on.

We don't know much about the mother except that she is eighteen and worked as a nurse's aide here in Topeka. The past four months she has been in a home for unwed mothers. The father is listed as unknown.

So her birth mother had worked as a nurse's aide! Hastily Deni scanned the next sheet. She was trembling; she might find out everything if she could just control herself.

The young mother's father is a minister. The family is very upset about the pregnancy and favors the adoption. They live close by in the little town of Eudora.

Eudora! Deni was stunned. She had asked her mother once where her birth mother had been from, and her answer had been so vague that Deni had assumed she didn't know. But Eudora was only forty-five minutes away! She had seen the Eudora sign hundreds of times on their way to Kansas City.

Her grandmother stirred in her sleep, her eyelids fluttering several times. Deni quickly scanned the rest of the letter.

All it talked about was a baby shower her mother's friends were planning and the details of the nursery redecoration. That was all there was.

Deni hurriedly folded the letter and put it away. Then she turned off the light and sat back in the chair in the darkness, trying to think.

Why hadn't her mother told her that her birth mother came from a little town so close to them? What was she hiding? Was she afraid that Deni would try to go find the woman? Did the woman still live there?

That must be it! In Eudora, Kansas, less than an hour away, was the woman who had given birth to her! Was the woman looking for her, wondering what had happened to the baby she had given away? Was she, like Deni, always looking at faces in crowds, looking for someone with her own features, thinking she might find her? Had her family forced her to give up her baby against her will? Did she need Deni as much as Deni needed her?

As the rain pounded on the window, Deni slipped into her old daydream, the same one that she had fantasized, with slight variations, since she was old enough to understand what adoption meant. . . .

In her dream Deni was cold, tired, and hungry. Suddenly she encountered a beautiful woman, a woman who looked like a movie star and was richly dressed in satin, lace, and furs. The woman recognized her instantly, and she held out her arms to Deni and said, "At last I've found you, my darling! I've been searching for you since the day you were born and taken away from me! All I need is you! Come live with me. Your lovely room is waiting for you, and I will love you always and make it up to you for being adopted. We will never be apart again."

Then the two of them walked off together to live happily ever after. Her mother, Chuck, and her grandmother never appeared in the fantasy. It was as though they had ceased to exist. Because in her fantasy, Deni finally had a real family—her own mother. And Deni felt as if she had found her real home.

Chapter Six

Deni lay on her bed, lost in thought. It was still raining hard outside, and her room had grown chilly. She shivered and put an arm around Sam. He was curled up on her bed taking a nap, one paw resting on an unopened letter from Lori that had arrived in that day's mail. An old record played softly in the background, automatically restarting when it ended. It had been playing for over an hour.

Her mother would be home soon from her after-work visit with Deni's grandmother, and then it would be time to start dinner. How could Deni pretend that everything was the same? Perhaps she could calmly confront her mother, tell her about reading the letter, and say she wanted to meet her birth mother. Then she could ask for her birth mother's name.

Deni knew that being direct wouldn't work. Her mother would get upset, even though she would probably act calm and controlled. Deni knew from past experience that her mother would feel threatened. She could almost hear her saying, "Why do you need to meet her? Don't you know how much I love you?"

If Deni tried to explain that it wasn't a question of love but a question of needing to *connect* with another person, her mother would probably say something like, "I've always loved you as my own." And that would end the conversation because how could Deni hurt the one person who adopted her and was still giving her such a good life?

But Deni was hurt now, too. What right did her mother have to keep information from her—not to tell her that her birth mother lived nearby? She had a right to know that, and her mother should have told her. This was *her* life, not her mother's.

Deni felt a flicker of guilt; she knew she should feel more gratitude to her mother than she did. Her mother had never expected gratitude, that wasn't it. But Deni knew that she could have spent her life in an orphanage or could have been adopted by someone who wouldn't have been a good parent. She shuddered to think about that. There were some terrible parents in the world. Plenty of newspaper stories proved that. Deni had been lucky.

OK, so maybe she would forget the whole thing. Why search for someone who had rejected her at birth? Why have anything to do with someone who could give up a baby? Why stir up the past and perhaps cause trouble in the present?

"Because I have to *know*," Deni said out loud. "Good or bad I have to know. And it doesn't have anything to do with my adoptive mother and how I feel about her. I just need to see my birth mother and know that she actually was—*is* a real person. I want to touch her. Just once will be enough. This is something I need to do for *me*."

Well, if that was the real reason, then there was no reason for her mother to know what Deni was doing, she reflected. She would find her birth mother—and maybe her birth father, too—on her own, and her mother wouldn't have to know about it or be saddened by it.

Deni got up and walked over to her dresser. She *could* find her. Eudora was a small town, and her birth mother's father—Deni's grandfather—had been a minister. People would remember. It was even possible that as soon as she got there, someone would tell her that she looked like so-and-so, and she would find her birth mother with no trouble at all. Maybe they would even run into each other on the street!

"When I find her," Deni said, staring at her reflection in the mirror, "I'll know who I look like, and I'll know all about myself. No more mysteries. No more wondering all the time. I'll finally have all the answers."

Then, when she turned eighteen and was given her original adoption papers, she would tell her mother that over a year before she had found her birth mother and they had become good friends and—Deni couldn't think through that one. She would just have to see how it all went. Her mother might not be able to handle the knowledge that she had not only found her birth mother but also had become friends with her.

Deni squared her shoulders. For now it was best not to say anything to her mother and simply go through this on her own. The rest of it would have to be worked out one step at a time. *Above all*, Deni would protect her adoptive mother from hurt. That was only fair.

Protecting her—that would mean keeping a secret from her, and they had always been so open with each other. Well, her mother had kept a secret from her for a long time; so Deni could justify her secret. She felt better having made a decision.

Deni picked up the letter from Lori and sat down at her desk to read it. It was written on bright purple stationery, and in the upper right-hand corner Lori had drawn an odd little creature wearing a T-shirt that said "Nerd" on it. She started reading, trying to concentrate on the words.

Scott asked me out! I can't believe it! He actually came over to our cabin and asked me to go into town to a movie! I thought my dad was going to say no, but then he said that since Scott's family would only be in the camp a few weeks that I could go ahead, and we did and it was neat! We held hands the whole time, and on the way home he ...

She reread the paragraph, trying to concentrate. Scott had asked Lori out. That was nice since that was what Lori wanted, and Deni tried to feel happy for her. But then Lori had always had a way with boys. Deni was the one who botched things up—obviously she had completely turned off Mike. Lucky Lori. Her parents had divorced when she was little, and she still felt a lot of pain from that, but at least Lori knew who her real parents were.

Deni laid the letter aside. Maybe later she could read it and write an answer. She picked up her sketchbook and absently drew a sketch of a woman holding the hand of a small child. She stared at it, then tore out the sheet and threw it away.

She flopped down on her bed, staring out the window at the rain. Sam moved over next to her, purring in her ear, ready to snuggle. She slowly petted him. "I've got to get myself under control, Sam. I think I'm going bonkers. Now I'm starting to draw *pictures* of this phantom birth mother of mine," Deni said in a low voice.

Deni flipped over on her back and stared at the ceiling. She needed a plan for finding out information about her birth mother in Eudora: positive, concrete steps. It was possible that they would simply run into each other, but she couldn't count on it. She had to go into the town with some pretense for seeking information about the family. Then, once she had found someone who knew them, the rest would be easy.

The phone by Deni's bed rang, startling her back to reality. It was probably her mother telling her she had been delayed and to go ahead and start dinner. She answered it on the second ring.

"Hi, Deni, it's Mike."

For an instant her mind went blank. Mike! She sat up quickly, her heart pounding. "Hi!" she said. Relief flooded through her. It was Mike!

"I was out on assignment all morning, so I didn't get to talk to you at work. Just wanted to tell you I had a nice time Saturday."

"Oh, me, too," she said. She smiled at the receiver. "I—I almost called you yesterday to tell you so."

"I wasn't home." He paused. "Did you get the sailboat sketch done?"

"I'm working on it," she said. She reached over to flip her sketchbook to the page with the half-drawn boat on it. She eyed it critically. "I still need to do a lot of work on the sail. I can't remember the detail of how it was attached to the mast."

"You need a photo to work from."

"Do you have one?" she asked hopefully. If

he did, he would have to see her to give it to her.

"I took several shots of the sailboat you were drawing, and at least one of them was a close-up. That might help. I'll get the film developed tomorrow," Mike said easily.

Deni felt herself starting to relax. He asked about her grandmother, and she told him about the latest letters they had read together. As she talked, she felt all her other worries fall away.

Deni told him she had gone to see her brother and his wife Saturday night and had stayed to watch a "Dynasty" rerun with them. "None of us had seen it, so we placed bets with each other about how it would end," she said.

Mike laughed. "Heather does the same thing," he remarked.

"Heather?" She felt her stomach do a flip-flop.

"Haven't I mentioned her?" he asked casually, though Deni thought she detected caution in his voice. "She's—a friend."

"Do I know her?" she asked, afraid that her voice sounded weak and far away.

"Probably not. She goes to Harding High. She'll be a senior," he said.

Something was starting to click. The image of the sexy blond focused before her eyes and was starting to get a face. She knew who Heather was! Heather. Cheerleader, model, clerk at The Sassy Q clothing store. Petite, blond, well-built, beautiful. Heather and Mike,

Mike and Heather. She knew she had seen them together. The perfect couple. And Deni? She could almost hear his comment to Heather: "Just a nice friend to spend a Saturday afternoon with while you're working. Nothing more."

"I know who she is. And she's—a good friend?" Deni tried to keep her voice even.

"Yeah," he said quickly. "I was calling to see if you'd like to go to a movie Friday night. I figured it was my turn to ask *you* out," he teased.

Deni could hardly believe what she was hearing. "But Heather—I mean, sure! I'd like that," she managed to say, hoping her voice was steady.

She heard him chuckle. "Good. I probably won't see you at work before then. The camera crew will be on location all week. Along with the adoption series, we're starting some new spots on Topeka industrial plants. It's a lot of work. Your brother keeps us busy. But I'll see you Friday night for sure," he said.

Deni said goodbye, and they hung up. She stood up on the bed, hugging herself. Then she grabbed her pillow, jumped on the floor, and danced around the room. "He asked me out!" she sang to the alarmed cat, who was sitting up, watching her warily. "He likes me! He asked me out!" She grabbed Sam and held him up in the air, swinging him around. Sam looked worried and began to wriggle frantically, finally jumping out of her arms and retreating under the bed.

A movie! That meant a dark theater and holding hands. That was much different from going to the regatta in the afternoon. But what about Heather? Was Mike with her on Saturday night? What did he mean when he said they were "friends"?

The phone rang again. "Hello," Deni said, her voice singing.

"It's Mom, Deni."

Deni knew instantly that something was wrong. "Mom?"

"It's your grandmother. She's had another heart attack. The ambulance is here at her house now. You'd better meet me at the hospital."

Chapter Seven

"How's your grandmother?" Mike asked, a concerned expression on his face. He instantly returned his eyes to the road, signaling his turn onto Kansas Avenue as he neared the downtown movie theater.

Deni shook her head. "She's—holding her own, I guess. The official term is 'resting comfortably,' whatever that means," she replied.

"I know you weren't sure about going out tonight," Mike said. He glanced at her. "It'll be good for you to think about something else for a while."

Deni had gotten home from the hospital just minutes before Mike arrived to pick her up for their Friday night movie date. Since her grandmother's second heart attack on Monday, everyone in Deni's family had spent as much time as possible at the hospital. Most of the time her grandmother wasn't even aware of their presence.

"If I seem a little quiet tonight, you'll know why," she said apologetically. "I have trouble keeping my mind off her. It's so hard to see her like this. Her first heart attack was mild, and the doctor let her stay at home. But now . . ." Deni's voice trailed off, and she shrugged. "We don't even know when she'll get out of intensive care," she added after a pause.

The first time Deni had visited her grandmother at the hospital, she became sick to her stomach. Other visits hadn't made it any easier. In spite of the many hours she had spent at the hospital during the past week, Deni still had to fight crying every time she went into the ward. Her grandmother looked so fragile, hooked up with tubes to machines that hummed and bleeped.

Every time she visited, Deni had hoped her fear wouldn't show in her eyes as she stood next to her grandmother's bed. Deni had held her grandmother's hand and talked to her soothingly, even though her grandmother really couldn't answer back. It was hard for Deni to watch, but she didn't know what else she could do. Her grandmother, once a strong, vital woman, now lay sedated, hardly able to talk, her eyes glazed from medication.

Mike interrupted Deni's thoughts, bringing her back to the present. "I lost my grandfather two years ago," Mike said. "He died unexpectedly. In his sleep. Everyone said it was a blessing, but—"

"But what?" Deni asked.

"Nobody got to say goodbye. That's hard to

get over. We all had things we wish we could have said to him. Especially my father," Mike said soberly.

Deni was quiet for a moment. Then she said, "I hadn't thought about that. You're right—and yet, if you purposely say goodbye, then you're telling the person that you think they're going to die." She looked out her window, thoughtful. "But that's still better than no goodbye. Now that I think about it, my grandmother probably knows that. Every time she ever said goodbye to me, she always added the words, 'I love you.'" She gave Mike a weak smile. "Gram can say those words more easily than most people."

"I wish I could meet her," Mike said.

"She wants to meet you, too," Deni said. Mike smiled at her.

By the time they got to the theater, Deni was glad she had kept the date. Mike was comforting to be with. She had shed a few tears in front of her mother but had tried not to burden her with her grief and fear. In times of crisis, Deni's mother withdrew into herself, and Deni tried to leave her alone. Chuck and Kara were wrapped up in their own concerns. So talking to Mike had provided her with an unexpected outlet.

When Mike took Deni's hand during the movie, a tiny thrill ran through her. Maybe she wasn't just a friend to him; maybe Heather wasn't his girlfriend anymore. She tried to concentrate on the movie, but her head was swimming. So many things had happened in the past week: meeting Mike; her grandmother's heart attack; her new hope of finding her birth mother. The summer wasn't turning out to be as quiet as she had expected.

As they walked out of the theater, still holding hands, Deni turned to Mike. "How about some popcorn and television at my house?" she asked. "It's still early."

"I have a better idea," Mike replied. "I'll show you the lake where my cousins live. That's where I sail with them. It's about ten miles outside Topeka."

Twenty minutes later they were at a small lake with a few houses dotted along its shore. Mike showed her his uncle's house and the dock where they launched the small sailboat. Then he drove to the opposite side of the lake and parked the car. They got out and walked down a gentle slope to the water's edge.

The surface of the lake shimmered in the moonlight. Along the edge of the opposite shore the lights from the few houses cast reflections in the water, which danced in the ripples of the gentle tide. Except for the distant sound of a small motorboat whisking night fishermen over the lake and the occasional splash of fish breaking the water's surface, all was quiet.

Mike and Deni sat at a picnic table only a few feet from where the water lapped the bank. After a few moments Mike reached over and took Deni's hand. She smiled at him and returned the gentle pressure of his grasp. They sat in silence, and Deni once again savored the freedom to be herself with a boy. She didn't need more time to know how much she liked him. *But,* she thought, *there is one thing I'd like to know more about him— Heather.* She shook the thought away, afraid to let it ruin such a beautiful evening.

"When I was little," Mike said, breaking the silence, "I hated being by myself by this lake. Every fish that jumped scared me, and at night, I was sure that there was someone in the woods, right behind me, who would jump out and grab me."

"So what did you do?" Deni asked.

"For a long time I just hoped I would be able to outrun the person. I was constantly looking over my shoulder in one direction for hours."

"But that meant the person could jump out from another direction," Deni protested, laughing.

"Then you understand the problem!" Mike said, joining her laughter. "When I finally figured out that no matter where I turned, there would always be someone lurking behind me, I gave up. Pretty soon I got over being scared."

"Kids are funny," Deni said. "In the house we lived in when I was young—before my dad died—there was this one tiny room at the top of the stairs. I hated that room until I was about five or six."

"Why?" Mike asked.

"I don't know," Deni answered. "It wasn't much bigger than a closet, and my parents didn't use it for anything. Then one day I told my mother I wanted to have an art gallery so I could show off my paintings and drawings. You should have seen *those* works of art!"

"I would have liked to," Mike told her, squeezing her hand lightly.

"Anyway, my mother went into my bedroom and gathered up all my drawings and hung them up in that little room. When my dad got home, she took him on a tour of the 'gallery.' She left them there, and every time I had a new batch of drawings, she'd add them to the collection," Deni said.

"So you didn't hate the room anymore."

"I couldn't! I even bragged about it during show-and-tell at school," Deni finished.

She lapsed into silence again. Mike still held her hand. It was such a perfect evening, Deni thought, except for that one tiny doubt that kept nagging at her. She tried to ignore it, but she couldn't. If Mike was enjoying the date as much as she was, then what could Heather mean to him? Yet Deni wasn't sure that she really wanted to know. After all, if he still liked Heather and he was with Deni, what kind of a boy was he? She didn't want to pressure him, but it troubled her that he might be seeing someone else, and she didn't know what that someone else meant to him.

Deni shivered slightly in the gentle breeze, the tall grass cool against her legs.

Mike got up from the bench of the table, bent down and picked up a stone, then skipped it across the water. He was standing with his back to her. He cleared his throat. "Deni, you want to know about Heather, don't you."

How had he *known*? Deni didn't know what to say. "Well, I—it's really none of my business, Mike," she began hesitantly. But that wasn't true! She most certainly *did* want to know about Heather! Deni waited, and for several moments he was silent.

"I want to be honest with you," Mike said.

"I'm glad—"

"I've been dating her for a year now. But lately—I don't know how to explain this. I haven't had any luck trying to explain it to her. It comes down to my needing space. Some time to test my feelings," he said. He was quiet for a moment. "She expects too much from me—more than I'm willing to give her. We had a date last Saturday night after you and I had been to the regatta. I tried to talk to her about everything, but she just got upset. That's part of the problem. She's very possessive."

Deni spoke carefully. "Look, Mike, I understand. Really I do. You need time. As far as I'm concerned, you and I are just friends." She kept her voice light, but her heart wasn't in those last words. She liked him *so* much! "I can always use another friend," she added.

"I just don't want to hurt you," Mike said, turning to her. He took her hand again. For a moment she thought he was going to kiss her; then he looked away.

Mike let go of her hand as he sat back

down on the bench next to her. Deni waited. It was his move.

"Did Chuck tell you about Crystal?" he asked suddenly. Mike was deliberately changing the subject. She wasn't going to find out any more.

"Crystal? Is she the next child in the adoption series?" Deni asked, trying to keep her voice casual. She hoped he couldn't tell that she was upset. How could she be just friends with a boy she was falling in love with?

"Right," he replied. "I thought maybe he would have told you about her. She's seven, one of her arms is deformed, and she's been living in foster homes since she was born. We had a hard time filming her. She's not a happy kid—has a real chip on her shoulder. It's hard to blame her, but with her attitude problems it may be tough finding a family for her."

Deni felt her interest growing. "How did she act? Did she cry?" she asked.

"She just—she just wouldn't smile, and she didn't say much. She wasn't antagonistic, exactly, but she wouldn't cooperate with us. She sort of stared at her shoes and wouldn't do anything for the camera."

"Maybe you scared her," Deni commented.

Mike looked surprised. "Why? She knew why we were there. She knew we wanted to help her find a real home."

"But, Mike, think what it would be like to be in front of a television camera knowing that how you behave could determine whether someone watching would be interested in giving you a home. That would scare anyone! She probably thinks nobody's ever adopted her because of her crippled arm. Poor kid. I wish I'd been there," she said, almost to herself. "I might have been able to help her understand."

Mike looked upset. "You're right. None of us thought about any of that."

"Don't blame yourself," she said. "Let's just hope we get some calls at the station next week after the tape is shown on TV. I got several last Tuesday and Wednesday after Freddie was on. There's one couple who's already been to visit him."

"I heard about that," Mike said. "It's nice to be part of helping a kid like Freddie."

Deni looked at him warily. "As long as you don't get self-righteous about it," she said. "If you act that way around someone like Crystal or Freddie, it could make them feel worse than ever."

He started to say something but then stopped. "You're the adoption expert. I bow to your expertise *and* promise not to get too self-righteous," he added. He looked at her. "Is being adopted really so bad, Deni?"

Deni glanced at him. What did he mean by that? Was he making fun of her? But all she detected in his voice was curiosity. No sarcasm.

"I don't know what you mean," she answered honestly.

"I just wondered, that's all." He smiled at

her. "I don't mean to pry, but it must be—well, kind of hard to think that someone gave you away. I guess I'm not making myself very clear," he apologized. "It's just that if you don't know *why* you were given up, you could spend a lot of time trying to second-guess what had happened."

Deni nodded. "I have a wonderful family, but sometimes I do wonder about my real background. Mike, I—" She broke off.

He looked at her, waiting.

"Can I trust you with a secret? I mean, the kind of secret that you absolutely can't mention to anybody?"

"You're talking to a former Boy Scout. Trustworthiness is my middle name," he said. Even though his words were light, Mike's tone was completely serious.

Deni took a deep breath. "I learned something from a letter at my grandmother's on Monday that might help me find my birth mother. I found out that she's from Eudora." She paused, then said, "I've decided to search for her."

Startled, Mike sat up straight. "What do you mean?"

"I mean I think I can find her. And I'm going to. The moment I saw that letter I knew I was going to search. This is my chance to learn about my past, and I'm going to take it."

Deni told him about the letter, getting more excited as she spoke. She and Mike were going to be friends, and Deni needed a good ally for her search. "I'm going to drive over to Eudora on Monday after work," she said. "I'll tell my mom I plan to go to the park to do some sketches. I do that all the time, so she won't be suspicious."

Mike stood up and walked a few steps away from her. He turned and looked at her. "Have you thought this over? Do you know what you're doing?" he asked. He sounded like a lawyer cross-examining a witness.

"Yes! I'm going to find the woman who gave birth to me. I'm going to meet her and get to know her. Maybe we'll even become friends."

He shook his head as if he were trying to take in Deni's words. "I can understand that you're curious, but shouldn't you think about a lot of things before you charge into this? Have you thought about what this is going to do to your mom?"

"I've thought about that a lot. She won't find out. I won't tell her," Deni said.

"Suppose she does," he said stubbornly.

"She won't. *I* want to make sure she doesn't get hurt," Deni said. She was surprised by his lack of enthusiasm. She had hoped he would offer his help. "Mike, even if my mom did find out, she would just have to understand. This is something I have to do."

"How do you think you're going to find this woman?" he asked.

"Well, it's a very small town. Just a few thousand people. I looked it up on the map. I'm going to drive over there and—"

"And?"

"Well, I'm going to *look*," she answered defensively.

"Oh," Mike said. His voice was sarcastic. "You're going to drive into town and look. You'll stop anyone you see who had brown hair and brown eyes and ask if they gave up a baby for adoption, and of course you'll instantly run into the right woman."

Deni tried to keep her voice even. She didn't want to show her irritation. "OK, so maybe I won't just find her, but it's a small town. I'll ask questions. I know the birth date and the place, and I know my birth mother's father was a minister. That's a lot to go on. The only thing I need is a birth certificate, and my mom's already told me she'll give me my adoption papers and my birth certificate when I turn eighteen."

"So just tell her what you learned and ask for them now," Mike suggested.

"I *can't*. She isn't one of those people who can be matter-of-fact about this. She's just not that way. Besides, she has too much to think about right now with my grandmother," Deni reminded him.

"Then why don't you just shelve this until you're eighteen? I don't know when your eighteenth birthday is, but it can't be more than a year or so away. Then you'll have the information you need," Mike said.

Deni looked at him. "Mike, a year is too long! Think of everything that can happen in a year! One month ago my grandmother was a healthy woman. Since then she's had two

100

heart attacks. I need to do this *now*. I don't want to wait. This way I'll have a whole extra year to get to know her. Think about it! Wouldn't *you* feel the same way? I want to know who I am!" The tone of her voice was harder than she had intended. Why couldn't Mike understand?

Deni waited for his response. Finally he stuck his hands in his pockets. "Does the offer still stand for popcorn at your house?" Mike asked. "It sounds good now."

"Sure," Deni said, trying not to sound disappointed. She had been wrong about him. He wouldn't help her. Suddenly she felt all alone.

Mike took her arm, and they started walking along the path toward his car. Deni was realizing more and more that people who hadn't been through adoption just couldn't relate to it. Lori, her mother, Chuck, her grandmother, Mike—everyone thought she should be happy with things as they were. But none of them had missing links in their pasts. No one understood her.

Deni could see Mike's car at the top of the path. Mike stopped and looked back at the lake and then at her. Even in the moonlight she could see the color of his eyes. He squeezed her hand and then, very gently, he put his other hand on her cheek and kissed her on the lips.

It was so sweet, so fleeting, that Deni felt a catch in her throat and thought for a moment that she might cry.

"Den, I know it's got to be tough. I'm trying hard to see it from your point of view," Mike said. He looked intently into her eyes. "If you need someone for moral support, someone to talk to about this, I'll be here. I really care about what happens to you."

He kissed her again. "Thanks," she whispered, her eyes bright with tears. They walked on, his arm around her waist. Deni felt exhilaration sweep over her. "Just for the record," she said, nudging him in the side, "my seventeenth birthday is August eighth."

Chapter Eight

On Monday Deni slipped into her chair at the station at eight-forty. Roberta wasn't upset about her being late. "Mr. Robbins won't mind this once," she had said. "He knows you've stayed past noon to finish up a piece of work or a phone call to one of our viewers. You don't need to punch a clock."

Deni wanted to run a comb through her hair, but then she decided not to take any more time away from her desk. A moment later she was glad she had stuck around; Mike's mother called.

"May I please speak to Mike Hogan? This is his mother," a woman said when Deni answered the phone.

"I'm sorry. They're taping right now, Mrs. Hogan. Can I take a message?" Deni answered. She wanted to tell Mike's mother who she was, to see if Mike had mentioned her. But she knew that she had to remain professional.

"Yes, please. Have him call me on his break, but let him know that he's been accepted into one of the scholarship halls at the university."

Mike had mentioned that he had wanted to get into one of those halls, to help reduce some of his room and board costs. "That's terrific," Deni said enthusiastically. "I'll have him get back to you as soon as possible."

"Thank you, dear. Goodbye." Mrs. Hogan said.

Deni put the receiver back on the hook and wrote out the message for Mike. As soon as the first morning rush of salesmen and appointments was over, she called the librarian and asked her to take incoming calls. Then she raced into the studio and headed straight for Mike.

He read through the message and clenched his fist in victory. "All right!" he said in a low voice. "All *right!*" he repeated.

"Come with me to get a Coke," he said. "If you can spare the time, that is." Deni nodded and followed him to the vending machines.

"This is great," he said, clutching the phone slip in one hand. "I can do my own cooking, my own cleaning—this is really going to help cut college costs."

"I knew you'd be excited," Deni said. "It looks like you're going to be needing those survival skills your mother taught you."

"I'm not sure if my chicken salad recipe is going to see me through four years of college," Mike conceded. "But it ought to at least get me through freshman year."

"Your mother sounds nice," Deni said.

"Oh, that's right, you talked to her. Yeah, she's pretty OK. Did you tell her who you were?" Mike asked.

"I wasn't sure she'd know," Deni answered. "So I didn't mention it."

"She knows. I'll tell her when I get home," Mike said. Deni tried not to let Mike know how glad that made her.

"I had another phone call," Deni said. "It wasn't as nice."

Mike's eyes looked troubled. "What?"

"Another viewer called—about Freddie. She wanted to know if adoptive parents would have access to each child's family tree. She said she wanted to make sure of his background before she considered taking him," Deni told him. "I *have* to give her name to the agency, but I made a couple of notes to go with it—just so they'll know to ask *her* all the right questions."

"I guess people can be really stupid sometimes, right?" Mike said.

"I had a teacher who had us make family trees," Deni said. "I did it, but I felt like I was borrowing a family. I guess it's valuable in some ways because it makes kids aware of all the generations that went before them, but that was a hard day for me. Even worse than going to family reunions."

Mike nodded in agreement. "I can see the problem," he said. "At our family reunions most of the talk centers on who looks like whom and stories about the ancestors. And when you get together in groups like that, nobody would even think that someone there might be adopted and feel disconnected."

"What's worse is feeling like an imposter, as if you've just sort of stepped into this family but you don't really belong and that everybody is just pretending to be nice to you but is secretly feeling sorry for you and regarding you as an outsider."

"Did anyone actually do that to you?" Mike asked.

"I can still remember a great-aunt clucking at me and asking me about school. Then she said something about how much I looked like so-and-so, and another aunt gave her a dirty look to *remind* her what she was saying. And suddenly this aunt got very quiet. It was an awkward moment."

Mike didn't say anything then. Instead he just gave her a quick, tender hug. She wanted him to kiss her, but too many people were around. She wasn't going to risk somebody telling Chuck.

For several moments Deni debated whether or not to mention that she was going to Eudora that very afternoon. She decided against it. She didn't want to answer all his questions again. She would tell him all about Eudora later.

Right after work Deni drove to the hospital. She planned to stop in to see her grandmother and then leave for Eudora.

"Gram? It's Deni."

Her grandmother slowly opened her eyes. Deni watched her struggle to focus, as though she had been adrift in another world and was just now coming back to this one. When she saw Deni, she smiled. Deni took one of her hands and pressed it between her own, trying to fight back to the tears welling up in her eyes.

"How are you feeling today?" She tried to make her voice a little louder than usual to help her grandmother understand her better. Her grandmother struggled to speak, her mouth working to form the words. She was sedated, and Deni could tell that it was an effort for her to stay awake. She spent most of her time in a heavy, drugged sleep.

"Fi—" her grandmother said, her voice barely a whisper. "I'm—fi—."

"You're fine? That's wonderful!" Deni tried to sound as cheerful as possible. If only she could keep from crying. She had to try very hard. She didn't want to upset her grandmother.

"You—look—so lovely," her grandmother said with effort. "I like blue on you."

Deni gently squeezed the shriveled hand she held. "Thank you, Gram. I know it's one of your favorite colors, and it's one of mine, too."

Her grandmother smiled slightly. "Yes," she whispered. She began to finger the colorful handmade quilt on her bed with her free hand, feeling the small squares and the stitches that held them together. "Where—" she began.

"Mom brought it from your house," Deni answered, guessing the question. Her grandmother had asked it several times before, always forgetting the answer. "Since it's your favorite one, Dr. Brock said you could have it on your bed. Now all you need is Belzy!"

At the mention of the cat's name, her grandmother looked concerned.

"Wha—"

"She's OK, I promise. We're taking good care of her," Deni said, quickly wiping away one tear that had escaped down her cheek. "Your neighbor Mrs. Jacobson feeds her every day and talks to her and pets her. You know how much Mrs. Jacobson has always liked her." Her grandmother looked pleased.

"I brought you something, Gram," Deni said. She held up a small watercolor painting on stiff parchment paper. Her grandmother struggled to focus on it. "Why it's—" She tried to make her tongue form the words, her eyes blinking rapidly. "It's—"

"Your baby roses, the ones on the porch trellis," Deni said, holding the picture close for her. "I'll ask the nurse if we can set it up on the nightstand so you can see it when you want to."

Her grandmother smiled and closed her eyes. Deni sat by her, still holding her hand. Next to the bed the monitor machine hooked up to her grandmother's heart beepeed steadily, sending its zigzag line of phosphorescent green shooting across the screen. A plastic bag filled with a clear solution hung above the edge of the bed, dripping continuously through a tube and into a needle attached to a vein in her arm.

She looked very tiny and fragile surrounded by so much paraphernalia, Deni thought. She watched the sleeping figure, her thin arms over the beloved quilt. The room was only steps from the nurses' station where her heart was constantly monitored on what looked like a computer screen. A nurse had shown it to Deni and had explained how it worked.

The fact that her grandmother had made it through an entire week since her major attack was a positive sign. It had been a week ago that day when Deni's mother had called to tell her to come to the hospital.

Margaret, one of the nurses on the afternoon shift, walked in just then. "That's OK, you can stay," she said as Deni started to leave. "She may be awake again soon. She comes and goes."

Deni sat back down. She wanted to stay in case her grandmother woke up again, but she also wanted to leave. She needed plenty of time for her trip to Eudora.

"Your grandmother is a spunky lady," Margaret said. "She's doing as well as anyone could expect her to. But she's worried."

Deni didn't understand. "You mean worried about her heart?"

"No, worried about your mother. Thinks she's taking all this too hard and will make herself sick over it."

Deni smiled and shook her head. "That's

just like my grandmother—to worry about someone else when she's the one who's sick. Will you tell her I had to leave, Margaret? I have some things I have to do this afternoon, but I'll try to stop back this evening."

"Sure," the nurse said. "Looks to me like she's in a deep sleep now anyway. I'll tell her for you."

Deni kissed her grandmother on the forehead. She thought about what Mike had said at the lake about his grandfather. "I love you, Gram," she whispered to the sleeping figure. "I love you."

She cried softly on her way to the parking lot. Her grandmother was not the same person she had been before her last attack. Everyone tried to be optimistic, but no one was talking about her going home very soon. There were no restrictions on how long her family could stay with her, but since her grandmother slept most of the time, there was nothing to do but sit on one of the chairs in her room. When her grandmother was awake, she had difficulty talking, because of the heavy medication, but it didn't keep her from trying.

Mrs. Lambert was spending as much time as possible at the hospital, going there directly from work and staying for several hours. She ate her evening meal in the hospital snack shop. Deni visited every afternoon and sometimes came back in the evening. Chuck stopped in right after work, then went home to check on Kara. She hadn't been able to come yet; her doctor had told her to take it easy and stay in bed until she felt better. Chuck often returned to the hospital later in the evening.

Her grandmother had voiced Deni's own fears about her mother. She was under a lot of pressure at work right then, and besides the hospital visits, she was stopping by her mother's house every day to make sure that the plants were healthy and to take the mail in. Deni had offered to do it, but her mother had said she didn't mind. Deni knew her mother wasn't sleeping well, either. When she had come downstairs on Monday morning, she saw an open book by her mother's reading chair. Mrs. Lambert had admitted to spending several hours in the night trying to read herself to sleep.

Deni unlocked her car and held the door open for a minute to let the heat escape. It was the first really hot day of the summer, with the temperature almost at ninety degrees. Doubts flitted across her mind. Maybe she should give up the whole crazy idea about driving to Eudora to search for her birth mother. Maybe she should wait until her grandmother was better. She could go home and sunbathe for a couple of hours. Or go to the pool. Jana and Kris would be there, and she could spend some time with them.

Deni shrugged off those doubts. She knew she would go through with her search. Ever since her grandmother's heart attack, Deni had felt more determined than ever to find her birth mother. She was afraid *not* to try. Maybe her birth mother wasn't healthy. Maybe she was going to move away from Eudora. Maybe she hadn't lived there for years. Anything was possible. If Deni waited it might be too late, and she would forever regret her lost opportunity. It was better to go now and deal with the whole problem.

There were so many things Deni wanted to know. For example, where had her art ability come from? If she were to learn that someone in her birth family was a truly great artist, wouldn't that inspire her to do even more and give her the self-confidence to set her goals higher? Deni couldn't shake the notion that her birth mother was someone very special—rich or famous or maybe a great artist in her own right.

Minutes later she pulled onto the Kansas Turnpike, driving east toward Lawrence and Eudora. She wished Mike were with her.

The drive to Lawrence was hot since Deni's car had no air-conditioning, but she was enjoying the scenery too much to really care. She had been over that section of the turnpike many times, whenever she went to Kansas City to shop or to Worlds of Fun or a special rock concert. But that day she looked at it with new eyes. Mike would be traveling back and forth over that road when he started at K.U. in Lawrence in August. That made it extra special.

That day the countryside was lush and green from all the rain. It was picture-postcard perfect. The rolling hills were covered with young corn and dotted with square white Kansas farmhouses. The vast expanse of sky was the truest of blues, with wispy clouds lazily drifting high above.

Twenty-five minutes after leaving Topeka she was driving through the hilly, tree-filled little city of Lawrence, past the entrance to the University of Kansas, and then out busy Twenty-third Street with all its fast-food eating places, grocery stores, filling stations, and finally Haskell Indian Junior College. And then she was on Highway 10 to Eudora.

Just outside Lawrence, Deni looked to the left to the low plain called the Eudora Flats with its patchwork quilt of farm fields. Over in the distance on her right was the imposing bulk of Mont Bleu, one of the sentinel lookout points during the Civil War because of its height. It was beautiful country. Eudora was just ahead; this was where she had come from.

If Lori had been home, Deni would have considered asking her to go with her. Would Lori have done it? She might have thought that the search was as unnecessary as Mike seemed to think it was. But Deni could have made Lori understand, and Lori would have helped her.

She missed Lori so much! By the time their letters got to each other, the news was always old. She had finally written Lori to tell her how happy she was to hear about her and Scott. A day later she had received a letter from Lori—she had a new boyfriend and couldn't stand Scott anymore.

Lori had always been that way. First one boyfriend, then another. Deni couldn't do that. She knew she wouldn't think of anyone but Mike.

But what about Heather? Deni wondered. She had no idea how much Mike saw her, or how often he called her, or how serious their relationship was. Heather was so perfect. She was beautiful and popular. How could Deni compete with her?

Deni saw the highway sign pointing to the exit ramp, and as she changed lanes, she felt her pulse begin to race. This was it! She was almost in Eudora. The day before she had planned what she'd do. The first thing would be to inquire about the ministers who lived there in 1969. She had already decided to ask the local librarian for information. The librarian would at least know who else she might be able to talk to in her search for information.

Deni had her story all ready. She would say she was looking for her father's long-lost relatives. They had heard that the family lived in Eudora—or at least they had been living there seventeen years ago. The father of the family was a minister. She wouldn't mention that a daughter had given birth to an illegitimate child unless she had to. That would be too embarrassing.

In spite of what Mike had said, there *was* a chance that she would simply run into her birth mother. Stranger things had happened. She smiled to herself. She could just hear them—she and her birth mother—being interviewed by a television newscaster about the experience of seeing each other on the street and immediately *knowing* who the other person was.

Deni turned off the highway. She was there! In her birth mother's town, the town that she, under different circumstances, might have grown up in. She let the feeling wash over her, slowing her car to a crawl as she looked at everything, trying to visualize herself as a child in that setting.

The first thing she saw on the edge of town was a baseball diamond, a swimming pool, and a grade school. They all looked tidy and cared for. She pulled over to the edge of the road and studied them.

This is where she would have gone to school and where she would have played as a child. The pool was crowded with children and teenagers—that could have been where she hung out in the summer.

But something was wrong. Try as she might, she couldn't picture herself there. What was it? Why did she feel so numb?

After all, she had come *home.* She was there to find her *real* mother. And the next few hours could change her life, forever.

Chapter Nine

Deni drove on, looking closely at the grade school as she passed it. The brick building was ordinary, a solid square Kansas school. What had she been expecting? Something out of a movie or a painting? But she had been so sure that everything would be familiar to her, as if she had seen it in her dreams. Instead, she was seeing a pleasant little town that was clean and tidy and respectable looking. A nice enough place to grow up in, but not very distinctive.

A woman with long, dark brown hair was walking toward her. Her heart pounding in anticipation, Deni slowed her car to a crawl and waited. "Excuse me—"

The woman smiled and came over to her. Now that was something that could only happen in a small town. No one in Topeka would come over to a strange car. "Need something?" the woman asked pleasantly. Deni saw that she was too young to be her mother. And her eyes were blue.

Deni asked her how to get to the downtown area, and the woman pointed the way. As Deni sped up, she felt embarrassed by her thinking that the first brown-haired person she saw might be her birth mother. If Mike had been with her, he would have laughed. She wouldn't tell him about it. He didn't have to know *everything* that would happen to her that day. Besides, he wouldn't laugh if she found her birth mother. He would have to be quite impressed.

She rounded the corner by a high school and drove through a two-block-long business district. Then she parked in front of the grocery store and watched people go in and out. It was so hot. Deni wiped the perspiration from her brow. A mother with short, curly hair walked in front of the car, and a brown-haired little girl was with her. *Maybe that little girl is my cousin*, Deni thought. *Maybe the woman is my aunt.*

This is crazy, Deni told herself. She needed to get out of the car and do something. The store would be cool. She went inside. Deni was nervous, unsure of herself. Her hands were unsteady, and she knew she must think through her movements carefully before doing or saying anything.

A woman with a solemn face stood behind the cash register. The grocery store was tiny, much smaller than any place Deni and her mother had ever shopped in in Topeka. The woman and the little girl were busy filling their cart. Maybe she could approach the woman with the story about looking for her father's cousin. But that wouldn't be a good idea. Deni needed some place more private for such a conversation. Her inquiries had to be discreet.

Finally Deni bought a package of gum from the clerk and asked if there was a library in town.

"Nice one," the clerk said. Her face was glum, unsmiling. "Around the corner that-a-way."

"And churches. Is there one special area of town where the churches are?" Deni added.

The clerk looked at her, scowling. "What church?"

"Is—is there one street where lots of them are?" Deni asked.

"I'll bet you're looking for the old Catholic church. It's real historic. Real pretty. Someone tell you about it? But you can't get into it. I think they keep it locked. You can ask at the new church, two blocks east of here."

Deni started to phrase the question differently, then stopped. Eudora was a small town. She could drive around and find the churches on her own. She thanked the clerk and left.

A dark thought struck Deni. What if her birth mother turned out to be someone like that clerk? Maybe Deni was better off not knowing. Maybe she should stop now.

No. This business had to be finished.

Deni drove around the block to the library and stopped in front of it. The building was small and fairly new. She didn't feel ready to go in right away. She would drive around for a while and see more of the town first, just in case the librarian needed to give her directions. "Maybe I don't want to do this," she murmured to herself. Now that she was so close, Deni was afraid. Sticking to her fabricated story about being in town to look for her father's cousin wouldn't be easy. Deni had never been good at telling lies. Lori had found this quality amusing. But Deni wanted, just for one day, to be able to lie convincingly.

She drove back down the main street and came to a small park. It was shaded and pleasant. On either side were some nice old homes. One of them reminded her of her grandmother's house. Another one was large and grand looking. It was kept up well; a new automobile stood at the bottom of its sloping yard. She studied it, taking in its rich details. Could it be that her birth mother lived there? Wealthy, isolated, lonely, wondering about the fate of the daughter she had given up at birth?

Deni stared at the house, willing the front door to open and a woman in her midthirties to walk out. Nothing happened. She waited several minutes, and then finally drove on, through shady old neighborhoods and past several churches. Which one? she asked herself.

After a half hour of circling, she turned back toward the main street and parked her car in front of the library. This was where her search had to begin. It was time to test her story. "I'm trying to find my father's cousin, a minister in Eudora who had a daughter who was eighteen in 1969 and worked as a nurse's aide in Topeka," she whispered to herself.

It wasn't enough. She should just go home.

Deni sat in the car, perspiring in the heat, trying to build up her nerve to go into the library. She was sure that people would think she was crazy. They would become angry.

"I need to do this," she mumbled. "It's right for me to do this."

Deni took a deep breath and slowly got out of the car. She must appear sophisticated and poised. Older. She was wearing bermuda shorts, a short-sleeved blouse, and knee socks. She wished she had worn a dress.

Inside the library the air was cool. Several people were there, reading books or browsing through the stacks. Nobody was at the desk. She waited beside it, and the cool air revived her. If the librarian was young, it wouldn't work. She would have to give up and go home.

"Hello, may I help you?" a woman asked. She had gray hair and silver-rimmed glasses. Her face was kindly, with laugh lines around her eyes. She looked like everyone's favorite grade-school teacher.

Deni gave her a quick smile and cleared her throat. "My name is—" She paused. "My name is Denise—Smith," she said, trying to look the librarian in the eye. She could almost hear Lori laughing behind her.

The librarian smiled at her expectantly.

"I'm—I'm looking for someone," Deni said. The librarian's friendliness was encouraging. "My family just moved to Topeka. From"—she tried to think quickly—"Texas. And my mother is trying to find a cousin of my father's. My father is dead. But his cousin lived here."

"I'll try to help," the librarian said, sitting down at the desk. "What was the name?"

"I don't know." That sounded stupid, she thought. Why wouldn't she know her father's cousin's name?

The librarian continued to smile. "You must know *something* about this cousin."

"We know he was a minister, but we aren't certain of which church. And we know"—Deni took a deep breath, trying to keep her voice casual—"he had a daughter who was eighteen in 1969 and that she—" There her voice faltered.

"Yes?"

"She worked in Topeka as a nurse's aide," Deni said in a rush.

"That's all? You don't know anything else?"

She opened her mouth and then closed it. "That's all."

The librarian began to consider various

names, thinking aloud. Deni looked around. No one was paying any attention to them.

"I'm sorry, dear," the librarian said. "I'm just not coming up with any ideas. Oh, wait a minute!"

Deni's heart jumped. "Did you think of someone?"

"Well, I can remember a Congregational minister who was here about that time, and he had daughters. Three, I think. Now what was his name?"

A small girl came to the desk with a stack of books. She stared at Deni. "Hi, Louise," the librarian said. "Look at all these books you're going to read! Excuse me," she said to Deni.

She stepped back while the librarian helped the child. The library was so pleasant that she wondered why more people weren't there. When the little girl left, Deni edged back over to the desk.

"Now where were we?" The librarian smiled. "Trying to think of a name, weren't we? Hmmm. If I remember right, it was something like Purdell or Peters. Maybe Pool. Something like that. Sort of a strange family—begging your pardon, dear, I know they might be relatives. Not social people, though. The minister was quite strict, and they didn't mix much in the community. Those girls mostly stayed together, loners as I recall. But none of them live here anymore. They moved away, I'd guess sometime in the early seventies."

"Would you know where—" Deni began.

"No, dear, I wouldn't. Now Reverened Schmidt has daughters, and they're all grown-up by now. I think one of them still lives around here, but I don't recall for sure. You know how it is." She smiled at Deni. "New people coming into town all the time to work over at the plant in De Soto, and it's just so hard to keep track of everyone." She looked at Deni. "Have I helped?" she asked brightly.

"Well, we need to find them if we can," Deni said.

"Got a big insurance policy to share?" the librarian asked. She chuckled.

"Something like that," Deni said, trying to keep her voice steady. "Actually, we need to find the daughter. It's very important."

"You might try Mr. Larson at the café," the librarian said. "He's lived here all his life and knows everybody in town. You try him."

"The café?" She looked toward Main Street. She hadn't seen a café there.

"Just around the corner over there," said the librarian, pointing. "You'll see it. No sign, but just look inside the window. Everyone knows where it is." Deni thanked her, then left the library.

Within minutes Deni was standing in front of a dilapidated café with a small lunch counter and a few tables inside. She went in and sat down. The table was sticky. She was the only customer there.

"Help ya, honey?" a heavyset, middle-aged waitress asked. She had platinum-blond hair and was perched on a stool behind the counter. Two noisy electric floor fans blew wisps of breeze in her direction.

Deni looked around. No one else seemed to be in the building. "Is Mr. Larson here? I need to talk to him."

"Gone fishing this week," the waitress replied. "He'll be back next Monday."

Deni tried to think. Next Monday! That was a whole week away. Now what?

"Something I can do for you?"

"I don't think so."

"You looking for someone?" she asked.

Deni smiled at her gratefully. "A family who used to live here. A minister who would have had an eighteen-year-old daughter in 1969."

"She graduated from high school that year?"

"I don't know. Wait—I think she would have graduated in 1968 because in 1969 she was working in Topeka as a nurse's aide."

"My daughter graduated in 1965. You say you don't know the name?"

Deni shook her head. "That's all I know. We need to find her. She's—a relative." It was getting easier to tell the story.

"Maybe it was one of the Schmidt girls. Deanna or Carla. Deanna must have been in that class. Carla's younger. Their daddy is still at the Methodist church. Old Reverend Schmidt is the Rock of Gibraltar." The waitress chuckled.

"And was there anyone else? The librarian mentioned that the Congregational minister had three daughters," Deni said.

"Well, I never knew them. Congregational? That don't sound right. Maybe Baptist. The only preacher's kids I remember were the Schmidt girls. That Deanna was pretty wild."

"Do you think Mr. Larson might know?"

"He will if anyone does. He don't forget no one. He's the town historian. Only everything's in his head instead of on paper." She laughed loudly. "But he went fishing. I'll tell him you were in," she told Deni.

"And tell him I'll be back," Deni said as she started to leave. "Next Monday if possible. Thanks. If you think of anyone else—will you be here next week?"

"Don't know. Depends on the old man. He sets the schedule. Don't worry, honey. I'll tell him you were here."

Deni started to leave, then turned back. "Do either of the Schmidt girls still live here?"

"Well, not Deanna, of course," said the waitress after a pause. "But Carla settled down real nice, and she lives—see the little side street right over there? Just turn left on it. Carla's in the yellow house."

Several minutes later Deni knocked timidly on a loose screen door, and a black dog began to bark loudly from inside the house. A skinny boy came to the door. "Is Carla here?" she asked.

"Ma! Someone's here!" he yelled loudly. A woman who looked about thirty came to the door. She was wearing jeans and a western shirt.

The woman looked surprised. "Hi. I'm Carla. You want me?"

As soon as Deni began her story, Carla interrupted and invited her into the house. "Jerry," she said loudly to the boy, who was listening to them, "you go get them papers delivered. Now!"

Jerry grinned at Deni and moved to the far side of the room. Carla ignored him. The whole house smelled of cooking odors. It was messy, filled to overflowing with furniture, newspapers, and children's toys. A television blared, but Carla ignored it. She smiled at Deni. "The daughter was about eighteen in 1969? Well, that could be my sister Deanna. What about her?"

Deni caught her breath, hardly able to believe what she was hearing. Was this it? Was Deanna her birth mother? Very slowly she asked, "Is—was she living in Topeka that summer?" she asked. She waited for the answer, her heart pounding.

The woman looked suddenly suspicious. "Why would you want to know that?"

"She's CIA, Ma," Jerry said. He was sitting near the television, still listening to them. Deni wished he would leave.

"Get out of here, Jerry!" the woman yelled at him, throwing a pillow at him and hitting him in the leg. "Now!" The boy didn't move.

When it was clear that the woman wasn't going to make him go, Deni decided to try another question. "Was your sister ever a nurse's aide? Could you just tell me that?"

"Not unless you tell me why you want to know," Carla stated. Her voice had grown cold. Deni was afraid she was going to tell her to leave.

"I—would prefer not doing that," she said softly.

"Is my sister in trouble?"

"Oh, no! Not at all!" Deni burst out.

"That's a first, Ma," the boy said and laughed.

"Shut up, Jerry!" She peered at Deni. "You're so young," she said. "Why would you want her?"

Deni sat up very straight. "Could I just ask you if she's living in Eudora? Really, there's no trouble. I just need to talk to her."

"She's not here now," Carla said, shifting her eyes. She looked uncomfortable.

"Just tell her Aunt Deanna ran off to Omaha with Mr. Hawkins, Ma. If you don't, someone else in town will. It ain't no secret," Jerry cut in.

Carla glared at her son. "I'm going to break your neck," she threatened him. She looked at Deni and shrugged. "Guess now you know," she said to her. "My sister took off. Left her kids with her husband, and now she's gone again. You sure she ain't in some other trouble? God knows she's got enough as it is." Deni sat quietly, waiting, trying to look as nonthreatening as possible. Carla looked like she was considering. "Okay, I'll tell you. She wasn't in Topkea in 1969. She was in Massachusetts. She—"

"Was in the nut house there," Jerry filled in, finishing his mother's statement. "Just tell her, Ma. Lots of people know about it." When he saw the look on his mother's face, he scrambled out of the room and ran outside, still laughing.

"It wasn't a nut house," the woman said to Deni. Her voice was defensive and full of pain. "It was just a place—for people with emotional problems. Deanna ain't no nut." Deni kept her eyes on her lap. This woman had her share of troubles. Deni knew she was causing her pain. But she had to ask one more tough question.

"But she wasn't—couldn't—have been in Topeka that summer working as a nurse's aide?" Deni asked. A wave of relief went through her as Carla shook her head.

"No way. I can tell you I remember real good when she went to Massachusetts. It was a pretty black day around here. But don't you go reminding folks here. That was a long time ago, and they forget after a while. No use reminding them. There's enough gossip about Deanna right now. Don't need to stir up the past. OK?" she asked.

"OK." Deni smiled weakly. She got up to leave. "I'm sorry if I—stirred up old wounds. Can you tell me—was there another minister in town at that time who might have had a daughter that age?"

Carla looked pensive. "Seems like there was. Can't remember the name, though. I was a few grades behind, so I didn't know all those girls. Try Mr. Larson at the café. He knows everybody."

Deni thanked her and hurried to her car. As she pulled out of the drive, she felt almost giddy with relief. That had been a dead end for which she was *glad*. She wouldn't have wanted to discover that Deanna Schmidt was her birth mother.

The other minister's daughter was still a possibility. Mr. Larson wouldn't be back until next Monday, so Deni would have to come back then. She needed to get home anyway. It was already four o'clock, and the drive would take her an hour.

As Deni drove back through the town and out to the highway, she tried to imagine what her birth mother must have been like growing up as a child in this community. But doing that was as difficult as trying to imagine herself belonging there: she couldn't. In her daydreams, when she was reunited with her wonderful, rich, glamorous birth mother, the setting was always vague. It was never clear *where* it was.

Deni strained to glimpse people in their yards or people walking on the sidewalks. She saw children and several teenage boys but no brown-haired woman. Then a thought struck her—a new thought, something that hadn't occurred to her before. "Maybe I got my brown hair and brown eyes from my birth father," she whispered to herself.

She pondered this as she drove along.

Trying to unravel her past was like trying to put together a jigsaw puzzle; it seemed as though none of the pieces were from the same puzzle. But that just made it more challenging. Deni would keep trying until every last piece fit.

Chapter Ten

Deni breathed a sigh of relief as she pulled into the driveway. Her mother's car wasn't there. If she had already been home, her first question would have been, "How did your drawing session at the park go?" And Deni hadn't even remembered to take her sketch pad with her. She could probably sketch something fast just in case the subject came up at supper.

But first she wanted to call Mike.

The mailbox was empty. That meant her mother had stopped home before going to the hospital. Maybe a letter had come from Lori. She would look after she had called Mike. Talking to him was the most important thing right then. Her head was swimming. She needed a sympathetic ear, someone she trusted to help her sort out what had happened. She needed Mike.

Deni didn't know what to make of her trip to Eudora. It had been unrealistic to think she would find some sort of fairyland with her beautiful birth mother waiting with open arms, and it was ridiculous for her to have thought that she might see her on the street. Deni could admit all that.

The real disappointment was finding a simple, ordinary little town and nice people who believed her made-up story. The mysteriousness of her daydreams had been destroyed.

Maybe Mike could help her put it all in perspective.

Had he been right after all? Would she be happier *not* learning the truth? No, it was a mistake to start thinking that now, just when she was getting close.

"Hi, Sam!" Deni greeted the cat. He followed her into the kitchen and then sat down by his food dish, waiting for his supper. "I'll feed you in a minute," she promised. "I have a phone call to make first."

Quickly, before she could change her mind, she dialed Mike's number. He would be just getting home from work. As the phone began to ring, an image of Heather flashed through her mind. Heather had waited on her a couple of times at The Sassy Q.

Deni caught a glimpse of herself in the kitchen mirror. She didn't have Heather's perfect figure and deep blue eyes, but she didn't have anything to be ashamed of. How could Mike be attracted to two such different types—a striking, blue-eyed blond, the other a slender, dark-eyed brunette?

"Must be my mind he likes," she murmured to the mirror.

By this time the phone had rung a half-dozen times. Deni knew she should hang up. *Please, Mike, answer it,* she thought. Then she heard a click.

"Hello?" Mike said breathlessly.

"Mike! It's Deni," she said, relieved. "I'm glad you're there."

"I just walked in from work. My mom must be out. What's up?" Mike sounded pleased to hear from her.

"Oh, nothing, I just—well, actually I—" Deni hesitated. What if he was critical of what she had done? "Nothing special," she said, feeling confused.

"Let me guess. You went to Eudora."

"Yes! I—"

"And you found her, right? And she's the mayor, and she's rich and famous, and she's dining at the White House tomorrow night and invited you to come along." He was teasing her, his voice friendly.

"Bingo!" she said and laughed. "How did you ever guess? Seriously, I think I'm getting close." She told him about her conversation with the librarian, the waitress, and with Carla. "There were two ministers at the time who had daughters the right age. I'm going back next Monday to talk to a man named Mr. Larson to see if he can help. I just know he can, Mike. I'm going to find her. She may not be right there in Eudora—somehow I didn't get the feeling that she was living there.

135

It didn't feel right. But I don't care where she lives. I'll go see her."

"Den—"

"Yes?" His voice was taking on that reproving, preachy tone again. *I don't want to hear this,* she thought.

"Look, I know it's none of my business, but do you want to know what I think?"

No, she said to herself. "What?" she said to Mike.

"I've already told you, for your sake and everybody else's, you've got to stop. Leave the past buried. Somebody will get hurt. You, your mother, or your birth mother. Maybe all three of you."

"Mike, you said the other night—"

"I know what I said, and I meant it. But I've been thinking about this. I can see so many problems. It could change your relationship with your mom. Do you know what could happen if—"

Just then Deni's eyes fell on a note in her mother's handwriting that was propped up on the kitchen table. She hadn't noticed it when she came in. She picked it up and scanned it quickly.

"Mike!" she gasped, interrupting him. "I just found a note—Gram is worse, and I was supposed to go to the hospital. You don't suppose—listen, I've got to go! I'll call you later!"

She hung up without waiting for his response, grabbed her car keys, and opened the door to the garage. Sam meowed loudly at her, and she stopped. "All right, all right," she muttered. Hurriedly she opened a can of cat food and gave him the whole thing—double his usual ration. Then she rushed out.

Only minutes later Deni pulled into the parking lot at St. Francis Hospital. She was out of breath when she turned the corner of the hallway to her grandmother's room. Chuck was standing outside the door and came to meet her. "You can't go in right now," he said, putting his hand on her shoulder. "Dr. Brock is with her."

"What happened?" she asked breathlessly, fear clouding her thoughts. "Where's Mom? How's Gram?"

"She's had another heart attack," Chuck said quietly. "She's old, Deni. Her heart had weakened so much from the first two attacks."

"Oh, no," Deni murmured. "Oh, no." She looked around, trying not to cry. "Where's Mom?"

"I talked her into taking a break and trying to relax for a few minutes. She's in the coffee shop. She just left. They aren't letting us in the room much, so there's not anything to do but stand around the hallway and try to keep out of the nurses' way."

Deni nodded, trying to calm herself. Chuck began to pace. She sat down next to the closed door and watched him. A feeling of guilt washed over her. Why hadn't she stayed there that afternoon in case her grandmother woke up? Instead she had been off on a wild goose chase looking for a ghost from the past. What if her grandmother died? She would never forgive herself for leaving. A nurse came out of the room and closed the door behind her. Deni and Chuck both looked at her expectantly, but she ignored them.

Chuck sat down beside Deni and put his arm around her shoulder. She wished her mother would come. She had to make herself think about something else. "How's Kara?" she asked after a moment.

She felt his arm stiffen. "The doctor ordered her to stay in bed. She's not feeling well. The new medication makes her nauseous, and it's still almost two months until the baby is due."

She patted his hand, something she couldn't remember ever having done before to Chuck. "The baby and Kara will both be OK," she said comfortingly. "Kara's done everything right—lots of rest, good nutrition, regular checkups—everything. The two of you are going to have a beautiful baby, and you'll be the best parents there ever were. I just know it," she said with conviction.

Chuck gave her a tight smile. "Thanks, Sis. I sure hope you're right."

The door opened again, and Dr. Brock came out. He nodded at them, his face somber. "You can go in one at a time for a few minutes," he said. "Be very careful to keep her calm. We have her heavily sedated, but you'll be able to talk to her a little bit."

"I'll stay here," Chuck said. "You go ahead."

Deni tiptoed into the room. Her grandmother lay on her back with her eyes closed, her heart monitor beeping steadily. A larger machine that had not been in the room that afternoon stood behind it. She wondered what it was for. The heavy smell of medicine filled the air. The blinds were closed, and the room was semidark.

She carefully took one of her grandmother's fragile hands. It was limp. "Hi, Gram," she said softly, fighting back the lump forming in her throat that made her voice feel tight. *Keep calm*, she told herself. *Don't cry.*

Her grandmother's pale blue eyes fluttered rapidly, struggling to open. She focused slowly on Deni, then smiled slightly in recognition. Her lips began to move, trying to form words. Deni leaned over her, straining to hear. Her voice was a raspy whisper, sounding as though it were coming from somewhere very far away. She looked intently at Deni as she spoke. "I—" Deni leaned over farther. Her ear was only inches from her grandmother's mouth. "Love—"

"Love?" Deni repeated, uncertain she had heard the word correctly. Her grandmother gave a slight nod and with effort added, "you."

Deni repeated the sentence, its meaning overwhelming her. This time it meant goodbye. Tears flooded her eyes and began to run down her cheeks, and she couldn't hold them back. She took a tissue from the bedside table and wiped her eyes with one hand, still gently and carefully holding her grandmother's hand with the other. "Oh, Gram, I love you, too," she said, her voice catching in her throat, her words broken and uneven. "You've always been the best grandmother in the world."

Deni looked at her. She seemed very calm and peaceful. She was blinking rapidly, her eyes watering. Was she crying? Deni couldn't tell. Her grandmother was trying to say something else, and again Deni leaned close. She made out the word "you," then "are" and, finally, "the best granddaughter."

She gently squeezed her grandmother's hand. But her grandmother wasn't finished. Deni concentrated on watching her grandmother's mouth as she struggled to form the words, putting all her effort into being understood. The sounds came in whispered gasps. "Best thing—ever for family—you coming—into—it."

A powerful, desperate wave of sadness rushed over Deni, making her head light and her knees weak. *Don't die, don't die!* she cried inwardly. *Don't leave me!* Gently she kissed her grandmother on the cheek and held both her hands. Her grandmother relaxed, the corners of her mouth slightly upturned in a smile as she closed her eyes. Deni choked on her sobs, her tears running freely down her face and falling on the pillow as she lay her head down beside her grandmother's and put her arms around her. "Goodbye, Gram," she whispered. "I'll always love you."

When the doctor came in a moment later

and tapped her on the shoulder, she made herself stand up. She turned, her face buried in her hands, and found herself in Chuck's arms.

In the hallway her mother embraced them both, and they stood together, united in their grief, their arms around one another.

Chapter Eleven

"This can't be little Denise! Why look at you! You're all grown-up! And, oh, my, aren't you pretty? I wish my Eddie was here to see you, why, he's just always had *such* a crush on you," Mrs. Dell said.

The heavyset woman gave Deni a bear hug, making her wince. "Hello, Mrs. Dell. It was nice of you to come," she said politely.

Mrs. Dell's face clouded. "Oh, honey, I wouldn't miss it. I just thought the world of your grandmother. She could grow the prettiest flowers of anybody I ever knew. I already know who you are," she said gushing and turning to Kara, who stood next to Deni. "Chuckie's sweet little wife. I remember seeing it in the paper when you two got married. I sent the clipping to my sister in Wichita. Now when is that baby due?" She patted Kara's protruding stomach.

"Not for another seven or eight weeks," Kara said pleasantly.

"You look pale, honey," Mrs. Dell said. "You just take care of yourself. I remember when my Eddie was born, he was so sickly." She threw her hands in the air and shook her head. "Nothing will wear you out faster than a sick one. You just take it easy."

"Good old Eddie," Deni said when Mrs. Dell moved out of earshot. "Do I remember him! The neighborhood creep. I really hated him. Being sickly was the least of his problems. I don't know who was happier when the Dells moved—Gram or me."

"I knew a kid like that in my neighborhood, too. A real animal," Kara said and laughed. They were standing in the hallway of Deni's grandmother's house, greeting the people who came in and left. "Looks like just about everybody who was at the funeral is here at the house. I'll be glad when today is over."

Deni glanced at her, concerned. "Are you sure you don't want to go lie down? Mrs. Dell was about the tenth person to tell you that you look pale—and you do."

"I'm fine," Kara insisted. "I'll compromise and sit on this chair for a while. I hate staying in bed so much." She sat down heavily. "At least my doctor let me come today. I think Chuck needs me."

Deni smiled at her. "You and Chuck are always so concerned about each other. He told me a few minutes ago how worried he is about you, and here you are, worrying about him! When I get married, I hope it's like that for my husband and me."

"Just make sure you marry someone as considerate as Chuck," Kara said. "Personally I'd say you have a good candidate out there helping in the kitchen." Mike had been at the house all day.

Deni giggled, glancing through the dining room at the kitchen door. "Mike's great, isn't he? It makes me sad that he and Gram never got to meet each other. I wish Gram could have lived long enough to see your baby, too."

Kara didn't answer Deni for a minute. Then she said, "I think I will take you up on that offer to rest for a while, Deni. I'll just go into Grandmother's bedroom—" Kara awkwardly got up from her chair. Her face was ashen.

"Are you OK?" Deni asked worriedly. "Should I go get Chuck? He's right in there in the living room, I saw him a minute ago, talking to Grandmother's cousins from Salina."

"I'm all right. Don't bother him now," Kara said, her hand on Deni's arm. "I'm just tired."

"No contractions or anything?"

"Oh, just a few. There's nothing to be concerned about. Just don't say anything to anyone, OK?"

"All right," Deni said.

Kara walked slowly down the hall to the bedroom and closed the door behind her.

Deni scowled and resumed her post by the front door. Poor Kara. The day had been hard on her, Deni thought. It had been hard on them all. The funeral, followed by the burial, had started at noon, and now, at four o'clock, people were still at the house. The dining room table was laden with food brought in by neighbors and friends. Deni could hear the sound of dishes being washed and dried in the kitchen and snatches of conversation from the living room and dining room. Mrs. Dell, she noticed, had cornered her mother in the living room.

Her grandmother had been loved by many people. The funeral service had been crowded. Deni thought the church had looked beautiful, with flowers everywhere, spilling off the casket and filling the front of the church she had attended most of her life.

Gram would have enjoyed how her house looks today, Deni thought. Everything sparkled. The pleasant, cool weather was a bonus. All the windows were open, and gentle breezes drifted in. Her yard and flowers were shown off to perfection. Deni and Mike had spent all their spare time the past two days cutting the grass and weeding the flower beds. Deni had also helped her mother and Chuck clean the house, and she had run errands.

Mike had been unbelievably helpful. Not only had he pitched in to help with all the work, but his calm, reassuring presence had made a big difference in her ability to get through the past few days as well as she had. She knew he truly cared about her. His sympathy was quietly given, but it was so genuine that she couldn't help but feel better when he was around.

146

The night before, he had come over to the house, and they had taken a walk. Without any hesitation she had begun talking about her grandmother and some of her favorite memories. He had listened closely, and when she told him about the last time she had seen her grandmother, on the day she had gone to Eudora, he had put his arms around her and held her when she had begun to cry.

She still had a hard time with the fact that Mike was seeing Heather, but she knew he was seeing her less and less and that he was still trying to sort out his own feelings. Tough as it was, she never brought up Heather's name. Neither did he.

"Hi," a familiar voice said, interrupting her throughts.

She turned and looked at Mike. "Hi. Who let you out of the kitchen?"

"I warned them that I would turn into an ugly toad at four o'clock if I wasn't finished. Said I wanted to see this very special girl I know," he said softly, smiling at her.

"Lucky me," she murmured, feeling a tingle go through her. She gave him a quick hug. "I think it's all just about over. People are starting to leave."

"Good." He perched on the arm of the chair Kara had been sitting in. "I just saw your mom. She really looks thin. Is she eating anything?"

Deni shook her head. "And I know she isn't sleeping well, either. Chuck told her that maybe she should go to the doctor and get

147

something to help her sleep, but my mom doesn't believe in that sort of thing." She rolled her eyes at him, and it made him laugh. "She still thinks that as long as she has a big breakfast every morning, all will be well in the world."

"But she knows that's not true if she isn't sleeping well."

"We took a walk early this morning, *before* breakfast, and I tried to bring the subject up. I didn't get very far. My mom is a tough person. Chuck reminded me that she was that way when my dad died, too. We—oh, good-bye, Mr. Stewart," she said to the elderly gentleman using a cane who had come up to her. "Thanks for coming."

"Your grandmother was a fine lady," he said, taking one of Deni's hands. "I knew both her and your grandfather for many years. Your grandfather and I went hunting together. He was a gentleman right to the tips of his toes. And your grandmother was a real lady. My late wife thought the world of her. Yes," he said, staring at something unseen on the wall, "everyone thought a great deal of her. And do you know, she looked much like you do now when she was young. Don't forget where you got your good looks!"

Deni assured him she wouldn't and gave Mike a tight little smile. "Can you believe that?" she said when he had left. "Gram had blond hair and blue eyes when she was young. I've seen pictures. I don't look anything like her."

"Age does interesting things to memory," Mike observed. "Maybe Mr. Stewart was just telling you that you had a lovely grandmother, and when he saw you, he thought of her."

Deni looked at him with wide eyes. "I think that's the nicest backhanded compliment I've ever received." She smiled.

"Don't let it spoil you," he said, winking. "It'll have to last you for a while. Where did you and your mom go on your walk?"

Deni shrugged. "Just around, through our neighborhood mostly. We haven't spent any time alone together in ages. I told her that before she died my grandmother had been worried about her. She just smiled and said to give her a few days to get used to the idea that her mother was gone and that she would be all right after the funeral. She's off in her own little world right now."

"And how are *you* doing?"

Deni looked into his eyes. She never got used to how beautiful they were. "OK, I think. I'm glad the funeral is over." She looked around. "I'm sure going to miss coming to this house."

He touched the etched glass in the hallway doors. "Yeah. It's really something," he said appreciatively. "You almost never see a house anymore that has this original glass and unpainted woodwork."

Deni smiled wistfully. "I've spent so many happy hours here. It kills me to think about someone else living here." She knew her mother couldn't stand that idea either. They hadn't yet talked about what would be done with the house.

A sudden image flashed through her mind. She was standing in the doorway of her grandmother's house—now her house—waiting to greet her beautiful, newly found birth mother who was coming up the front walk, roses in her arms. . . .

"Hey you two, where's Kara?" Chuck asked as he approached them. He looked tired.

"Resting in Gram's bedroom," Deni said. "It's been a long day for her."

Chuck's face was shadowed with concern. "I'm still not sure she should have come. She insisted. We've got to keep an eye on her, though. She's not as strong as she thinks she is. At least she's taking a break." He patted Mike on the shoulder. "You've sure been a big help today. Don't know what we would have done without you."

Mike shrugged. He looked pleased at Chuck's comment. "You and Deni were lucky to have a grandmother like that. What's nice is that you know it," he said simply.

Chuck nodded in agreement. "How did the taping go on Jake yesterday? Was it better than when you taped Crystal last week?"

"Like I told Deni last night, I think it'll come out real well. He's awfully shy, and because he has that speech defect he wouldn't say anything, but he's a cute five-year-old, and somebody ought to respond."

"Good," Chuck said. "I meant to tell both of you that the social service people received a lot of calls about Freddie, and they think they've already found a home for him. It looks positive."

"What about Crystal?" Deni asked. "She's old enough that it's going to be harder for her."

"That and the fact that she's not real friendly to people who talk to her," Chuck said, shaking his head. "I don't know what will happen. Didn't you say you got one strong inquiry on the telephone about her, Deni?"

"Yes," she said. "But the woman is single and older. We talked quite awhile on the phone. I gave her all the reasons why she should adopt Crystal."

"With you as the salesperson, the woman won't be able to resist," Chuck said, teasing her. Mike laughed. Deni smiled up at them both. It was fun to be talking to the two of them together. They were her two favorite males in the whole world. And with Mike around, Chuck seemed to talk to her more as an equal. Maybe they really would be able to be friends one day, instead of just big brother and little sister.

Hearing their laughter, Mrs. Lambert came over to them. Mike stood up and offered her his chair. She accepted it gratefully.

"Did you see how much food we still have left?" she said, motioning toward the dining room table. "Chuck, I hope you and Kara have lots of room in your freezer. Otherwise, I'll take some plates of cake and cookies to work with me, and you and Deni can take some to the station."

"We'll worry about all of that later," Chuck said. He glanced at the bedroom door. "Kara's lying down, Mom. Maybe you should, too. You look like you need it."

"I'm fine," she said quickly. "Only a few people are left now. It won't be long. I just talked to Mrs. Jacobson, and she said she would like to keep Belzy. The cat seems to be very fond of her, and Mrs. Jacobson certainly takes good care of her. I don't think it would be a real good idea for us to take her," she said to Deni. "She's an old cat, and Sam might get upset with her."

Deni sighed. Chuck had already said he couldn't take her because Kara was allergic to cats, and Deni knew that Belzy might have problems with Sam. "I guess that's the best solution, Mom. Mrs. Jacobson is real nice, and we can probably always go to visit her." She loved Belzy. The cat was almost as old as she was.

Mrs. Lambert smiled at Mike. "Thanks for the picture, Mike. I opened the package just before leaving for the church this morning, and I can't tell you how pleased I was!"

Deni looked at the two of them. "Picture? What are you talking about?" Mike looked embarrassed.

"It's of you, Deni. It shows you working on a sketch," her mother said.

Deni looked at him, surprised. "What?"

"Remember, I took it of you the day we

went to the lake," he said, a twinkle in his eye. "I thought your mom would like it."

"I'm going to put it on the mantel," her mother said, smiling. "I had no idea you were such a fine photographer, Mike. Deni looks so pretty in it—I know I'll treasure it."

They chatted for several minutes, then Mrs. Lambert went into the kitchen to check on the food. Chuck went back into the dining room to visit with the last guests.

Alone for a moment, Mike and Deni looked at each other. "How come you didn't tell me about the picture?" she asked. She pretended to be offended.

"It was for your mom. It just happened to be of you. I thought you'd seen me take it," he said, a sheepish look on his face.

"Don't you think you should have gotten my official permission?" she teased.

"Nope. Not unless you carry some sort of statement on your person at all times saying nobody has the right to take your photo without your authorization," he said with a straight-faced expression. Deni laughed. She looked away and then, almost shyly, glanced back at him.

"How are things with—"

"Heather? I thought you weren't going to ask me that," he said, his gaze steady.

"I know," she mumbled. "You can't blame a girl for wanting to know, though. Forget I asked."

Mike looked uncomfortable. "Nothing's changed. Most days I talk to her, and she knows about you. She had a date the other night with a guy who goes to Washburn University. At this point I would call us very close friends."

Deni tried to rationalize all this. She would need some time to think about it. Close friends was certainly better than dating. Just two weeks before, they were still dating. Why couldn't Mike just break up with a girl the way most guys did and never call her again? Deni sighed. Part of what made him Mike was the way he cared about and treated other people. But as long as he had any kind of relationship with Heather, Deni knew she was going to feel jealous. "I'm famished," she said, smiling at him. "Come with me while I make a sandwich."

Chuck walked into the hallway. "I'm going to check on Kara before—"

"Chuck?" The three of them turned toward the bedroom door at the end of the hall. Kara stood there, her face white and full of pain. "Chuck, I'm—we'd better go home." As they watched in horror, Kara began to slump to the floor. Chuck raced to her, catching her just as she fell.

"Deni!" he cried, panic in his voice. "Call an ambulance!"

Chapter Twelve

Deni rolled onto her side and propped herself on one elbow. She sighed and stared at the pink stationery scattered on the bed. Finally she picked up the sheet with "Dear Lori" penned across the top and studied it, willing herself to write something.

But she couldn't do it. The words wouldn't come. In exasperation she dropped the stationery and threw her pen aside. Finally she turned over onto her back and stared at the ceiling, listening to the soft raindrops fall against the window. How could it possibly be raining again? It had been the wettest June on record. Deni wasn't really concerned about the weather, though. She closed her eyes and let the events of the past few days wash over her.

She would never forget the long hours at the hospital waiting for the birth of Chuck and Kara's baby, John Christopher—the John for her father, Christopher just because Chuck and Kara liked the name.

Kara had been rushed to the hospital by ambulance. Her contractions were so strong that the doctors thought the baby would be born quickly. But the contractions weren't regular—they kept starting and stopping—and finally, at 2:00 A.M., her doctor performed a Caesarean section when the fetal heartbeat indicated that the baby was in danger.

Just before 3:00 A.M. Chuck had reported that he was a father. Deni smiled when she thought about the look on Chuck's face as he had relayed his news. He was concerned because the baby had been put on a respirator immediately, yet Chuck couldn't contain his exhilaration from having watched the birth of his son.

John Christopher weighed in at just under four pounds. The doctor had said that the weight wasn't bad for a preemie. But because of the baby's breathing problems, he would be hospitalized for one to three weeks and monitored constantly for any number of unforseen problems.

Kara would also have to spend extra time in the hospital regaining the strength she had lost in the last difficult month of her pregnancy. Kara looked pale and tired, but like Chuck, she was jubilant over John Christopher's arrival, and confident that everything would be fine. To Deni, it seemed ironic that Kara and the baby were in the same hospital where her grandmother had died.

Deni had been amazed by Chuck's transformation in the past few days. He was full of wonder at the miracle of his son's birth. And, as Deni had told Kara the night before, he was seeing his little sister in a new light.

It had started when Chuck suggested they go to the snack bar for a soft drink after Deni had visited the nursery. "As usual," Deni said to Kara, "he was being bossy and telling me how to take care of my car and everything. You know, acting like my *big* brother. So finally I looked at him and said, 'Chuck, do you give everybody unsolicited advice, or just me?'"

Kara had laughed. "I know just what you mean, Deni," she had said.

"Anyway, he looked surprised, and then he said, 'I do that a lot, don't I?' And I told him he did. Then he apologized and asked me if I'd like to go out to lunch sometime. I just about keeled over from shock!"

"But just think what a great father he's going to be for John Christopher," Kara had said, a twinkle in her eye. "He's all warmed up for fatherhood from years of practice on you!"

They had both laughed, but somehow the conversation with Chuck had been a turning point. Deni had longed for the day when he would stop being a bossy big brother and just be her friend. Maybe that day had finally arrived.

Now Deni sat on the bed and picked up the receiver of the phone, just to make sure it was working. If Mike couldn't call her, she would have to get in touch with him. The dial tone sounded normal. For some reason Mike was late getting home that day. He would call—he said he would.

Deni knew she was pressuring Mike, perhaps unfairly, to go to Eudora with her that afternoon to talk to Mr. Larson. On Saturday afternoon he had been at the hospital with her. They were standing in front of the nursery window watching John Christopher, who lay in his Isolette hooked up to all sorts of tubes and machines. He was so incredibly tiny and helpless looking. She had asked Mike to go with her to Eudora then. Deni knew she was going no matter what, and she told him that he didn't need to waste his energy trying to talk her out of it. Somehow, after witnessing all the pain and joy and care that went into having a baby, Deni was convinced more than ever that she wanted to find her birth mother. Not just for herself. Her birth mother had gone through a remarkable experience almost seventeen years before, and Deni wanted to let her know that she was willing to forgive her and be friends.

Mike had been reluctant to go with her. "I'll give you my answer Monday," he had said. "If you're going anyway, what I decide to do won't affect your plans. I've got to think about this."

Now it was Monday, and it was already after one o'clock. Deni had told him that she wanted to leave by two in order to be back by suppertime and avoid making her mother suspicious.

She picked up the stationery again. She had already written Lori about her grandmother's funeral and about John Christopher's birth. She had decided not to tell her about the search for her birth mother until it was over. It would be easier to tell her about it after Deni had actually met her.

The obvious topic to write about was Mike. Deni knew she was in love with him. A boy had never made her feel so good about herself! Deni felt happy and almost carefree when she was with him. The future held unlimited possibilities for them, and Deni was sure that she could accomplish *anything*. His quiet understanding, his sympathy, and his warmth had helped her through her grandmother's death and John Christopher's birth.

Deni sighed. Mike was still seeing Heather. He had, in fact, gone out with her on Sunday night. He had told Deni they were going to take a drive, and she had hoped that he would call her when he got back. But she hadn't talked to him since Saturday afternoon.

Lori was already on her third boyfriend of the summer. Mark was the latest—was, at least, according to Lori's last letter. No telling who it was by now, Deni thought, smiling. She began to write, asking Lori questions about Mark. But even those didn't fill up the page.

Deni doodled on a scrap of paper and stared out the window. The rain didn't look as if it would ever let up. The clock said 1:20. When would Mike call? If she didn't hear from him by two, she would *have* to leave without him.

The phone's shrill tones startled her. Deni picked it up on the first ring. "Hello?" she said breathlessly.

"It's Mom, Deni."

"Oh. Hi, Mom." She tried not to sound disappointed. Her mother almost never called her during the day. Was something wrong?

"I just wanted to check to see how you are," she said.

"I'm fine. No problem," Deni answered. Mike might be calling her right *now*! There was a pause at the other end of the line. Deni knew her mother still wasn't getting enough sleep and still had too many things on her mind. She went to the hospital every day and in the evenings wrote thank-you notes to everyone who had sent flowers and memorials to them. In her few free moments at work she consulted with a lawyer to wrap up her mother's legal affairs. "Well, I just wanted to check on you," she said. "I know your grandmother's death was hard on you, and everyone seems to be worried about me and how I'm taking it, and I'm not sure anyone is finding out if you're OK."

Deni smiled. "Really, Mom, I'm doing all right," she said, trying not to sound impatient. "I'm glad we all got to say goodbye to Gram and that she said goodbye to us."

"What do you mean, honey? Did she actually say goodbye to you?" Her mother sounded surprised.

160

"She told me she loved me. I think it meant the same thing."

There was silence. Then her mother said, "You just might be right. I'm sure after that last attack she knew she wasn't going to make it. Your grand—" Mrs. Lambert's voice cracked, and she didn't speak for a moment.

Deni waited, knowing her mother had something more to say. Mike would have to wait. Her mother needed to talk now.

"Your grandmother had a good life," her mother said after a minute had passed. "She was a loving wife and mother and grandmother, and she had many friends. I think she was ready to die and was grateful that she didn't have to endure a slow, lingering death. She was remarkable in so many ways. Did you know that when she was young, maybe twelve, her ambition in life was to be a rodeo rider?"

Deni laughed, remembering the story perfectly. "She said her parents were horrified and kept insisting that girls didn't do that. The first time she told me about how she used to hike up her skirt and practice trick riding on her horse, I didn't believe it was a true story. Gram was always so ladylike. But she told me a lot of times that I could be anything I wanted, *including* a rodeo rider!"

"She always enjoyed herself," her mother said. "And she always managed to see everything and everybody in a good light."

"I really miss her," Deni said softly. "I guess

until somebody's gone, you just don't realize what they meant to you."

"It's true," her mother replied. "One reason I called was to tell you that a realtor had contacted me about selling the house. I think we should go ahead. We won't have any trouble at all getting a buyer for it at a good price."

Deni felt a sudden rush of fear. "We just can't, Mom. We all love Gram's house too much to let strangers live there."

"But I'm really not interested into moving into it, Deni. It's too old and needs so much upkeep. I'm tired of taking care of a house. Somebody younger needs to do that now. It was a constant struggle for your grandmother to deal with it, and Chuck was forever over there doing something for her. There's really nothing to do but sell it. I just don't want the hassle of renting it."

Deni glanced at her watch. It was one-thirty. She tried to think. She needed to stop her mother from selling the house—but how? And she needed to get her off the phone so Mike could call!

A thought flashed through Deni's mind so quickly she almost didn't pick up on it. "Mom? I have an idea," she said excitedly. "Chuck and Kara love the house, and it would be perfect for them. I know Gram left the house to you, but Chuck and Kara could live in it and gradually buy it from you!"

"Oh, I don't think—"

"Mom, it'd be perfect! The day of the funeral Chuck was talking about how the south side would be ideal for a passive solar greenhouse. There's a good grade school for John Christopher just two blocks away. It's perfect, Mom! If they have another baby, the house they have will be too tiny for them. And this way, Gram's house will always be in the family," Deni said.

"Well, it's certainly a possibility," her mother said. Deni could hear the excitement in her voice. "But don't say anything to Chuck until I check this out, Deni. We all love that old house, but Chuck and Kara might not actually want to live in it. When I see Chuck, I'll discuss it with him. Deni, I'm so pleased! You might have come up with the solution! I'll see you after work," she added.

Deni hung up and smiled to herself. Things always had a way of working out. Deni was sure that her grandmother would have liked Chuck and his family living in her house.

Her hand was barely off the phone when it rang again. It had to be Mike!

"Sorry I'm calling so late," he said. "We were out on assignment and got delayed. I was afraid I wasn't going to get back at all."

"What have you decided? Will you go?" she asked.

The silence at the other end seemed to last forever. She heard him sigh. "OK," he said at last. "I'll go. I'll pick you up at two."

Deni said goodbye to him, put the phone back, and sat down on the edge of her bed feeling that old familiar tingle spread throughout her body. He was going with her! Everything was going to be fine.

Deni looked out the window. It was still raining. She got off the bed, brushed her hair, and selected a pair of mint green cotton drawstring slacks and a white T-shirt to wear, then put on her white sneakers. The slacks were a little dressier than jeans, but were they dressy enough? Mike would probably have jeans on, and it would look strange if she was dressed up and he wasn't. And her mother would wonder if Deni came home wearing clothes she normally only wore to work. The slacks and T-shirt would be a good compromise.

What if Mr. Larson wasn't at the café? Maybe he wouldn't know anything even if she did get to talk to him. Or maybe she would learn that the minister and his daughters had moved and that nobody had any idea where they had gone.

That line of thinking wasn't helping her at all. Maybe Mr. Larson would not only be there, but would be able to help her. Maybe her birth mother lived right there in Eudora and would be thrilled to death to find out Deni was there and wanted to see her.

Deni studied herself in the mirror. "Hello, Mother," she said to her reflection, smiling sweetly. "I'm your daughter—the daughter you put up for adoption." There would be the first shock, then uncertainty, and finally a tearful reunion. A reunion with her own true mother.

How wonderful it would be! Her mother lived close to Topeka, and they would be able to see each other often. After they got acquainted she would make arrangements for her two mothers to meet. They would like each other and feel grateful to each other for their shared role in Deni's life. Mike was wrong, thinking that what she was doing could lead to trouble for everyone. But how could he be expected to understand? After all, he didn't know what it felt like to be adopted.

She heard a car pull into the driveway and looked out her window to see him getting out. She loved him so! Deni had never expected things to work out so well. She hoped she would soon be facing her birth mother, with Mike—the boy she loved.

Chapter Thirteen

Mike pulled his car into a parking space directly in front of the small, anonymous café in Eudora. He turned off the engine, and they sat in silence, light rain falling around them.

The street was almost deserted. They could see several men drinking coffee inside the café. Deni recognized the waitress. Had she told Mr. Larson about her?

"I don't think we should go in yet," she said, beginning to feel nervous. "I can't ask questions with all those men in there."

Mike nodded. He turned on the radio, tried to find a station, then turned it off. The car windows were steamy from the humidity. The air inside the car was stifling, and Deni felt the first twinge of a headache. Mike looked hot. Beads of perspiration clung to his forehead.

They waited. The men showed no signs of

leaving. Mike tapped the steering wheel with his fingers.

"Let's drive around a little bit," he suggested after several minutes. "When we come back they'll probably be gone. They must be farmers rained out of the fields."

At the end of Main Street, they came to the small park. Deni pointed out the elegant old home overlooking it. "You'll laugh at me, but I was imagining the other day that my birth mother lives there. I suppose because it's the nicest home I've seen here so far." She smiled sheepishly at him. "I've pretty much given up on my fantasy that she's rich and famous and all—I don't think anybody here is, from what I've seen on the town—but I *wish* she lived there."

"Doesn't hurt to dream," he said simply.

They drove around the community, saying little to each other. She wanted him to like the town and was afraid he would be critical of its smallness and plainness. But Mike found everything interesting and commented that he should have brought his camera along. Deni tried to converse, but she soon was lost in her own thoughts, about her birth mother *and* Mike.

They had very carefully avoided the subject of Heather during the drive to Eudora. Deni had resolved not to ask about her. She knew Mike was struggling with his own feelings.

When they had to drive through Lawrence, he asked her if she would like to visit the K.U. campus with him sometime soon. "I want to show you Potter's Lake," he said. "It's right on campus, just two blocks from where I'll be living. You'd enjoy sketching it."

Deni had been afraid he would spend the whole time trying to talk her out of continuing her search, but that subject didn't even come up on their drive. She didn't want to argue any more with him. Apparently he had realized that he wasn't going to talk her out of her search and had decided to try to help her. She knew it was hard for him.

He had, however, mentioned Mrs. Lambert several times, but Deni knew that Mike just wanted to know how she was getting along. Deni was pleased that Mike liked her mother, but she didn't want to think about her when she was in the process of searching for her birth mother. As soon as Mike brought up the subject, she had changed it. He had seemd to finally get the message.

Mike drove around the town for a while, then returned to the same parking spot in front of the café. The men were starting to leave. It was still raining.

"We should be able to go inside in another minute or so," Mike said. "There's only a couple of them left now." He fidgeted in his seat. "I know I'm starting to sound like a broken record," he said after a moment, "but are you sure your mom's all right? I have a feeling you're not telling me something."

Deni gave him a sharp look. "Mom's OK," she said, annoyed. She knew she sounded defensive. "She's really tired, and she's upset over my grandmother and everybody's worried about the baby being so small, but my mom is strong, and she's going to be all right."

He didn't say anything else.

Deni turned her face toward her window. "Why are you trying to make me feel guilty?"

"I'm not."

"Yes, you are. Or else why would you keep bringing her up when we're here searching for my real mother?"

"Your *real* mother is back in Topeka," he snapped, anger in his voice. "The mother you owe your loyalty and love to is not the person you're trying to find today."

Deni stared out the window, blinking back sudden tears. She had never heard him use this tone of voice before. What was he saying? They'd been having such a good time. Why was he trying to get her to back out at the last minute by making her feel guilty? Maybe he wasn't the sympathetic, understanding person she had thought he was. She got her voice under control. "I'm going in." Deni glanced quickly at him. "Coming with me?"

He sighed and stared straight ahead. She was growing increasingly edgy. She wanted to go in. Mr. Larson would be able to help her. The search was more important to her than anything else in the world—even more important than Mike. She *had to know* her birth mother.

Deni looked at him, determination in her eyes. She would go without him.

Then he turned to her and put his hand get to work over hers. "OK, brown eyes, let's go."

She gave him a quick, grateful smile and got out of the car, running through the rain to the doorway. Mike was right behind her.

As they entered the small café, Deni started to tremble. She ignored the curious glances of the last two men who were paying their bill at the cash register and sat down at a round table in the corner. Her hands were shaking so hard she finally stuck them in her pockets. They waited in silence while the men settled the bill with the waitress. Deni didn't see anyone around who looked as if he could be Mr. Larson.

When the men left, the waitress walked over to them. She gave no sign of recognizing Deni. "What'll it be?" she asked briskly.

Deni gave her a quick smile, avoiding her eyes. "Is Mr. Larson here? We need to speak to him."

She looked hard at Deni. "Oh, yeah, I remember you," she said. "You're looking for family, aren't you. I told the old man about you. I sort of figured you'd be back." She looked at Mike. "This your boyfriend?"

"Well—yes," Deni said, embarrassed.

Mike winked at Deni.

"You're cute," the waitress said in a friendly voice. "Of course your girlfriend here ain't hard on the eyes, either. You make a nice couple."

Deni blushed. "Thank you. Is Mr. Larson—"

"He's in the back. I'll get him."

The waitress disappeared. Silently Mike and Deni sat amid the steady ticking of the old clock on the wall and the hum of the large floor fans. Deni stared out the front windows at the rain, and Mike picked up a menu and studied it.

Mr. Larson emerged from the back room. The waitress wasn't with him.

"Do something for you?" he asked. He looked friendly. His eyes were intelligent behind wire-rim glasses. An unlit pipe was stuck in his mouth, and he needed a shave. Deni told him the same story she had told the librarian. She thought the story sounded better this time. She added that she had already visited Carla Schmidt.

"A cousin, huh?" Mr. Larson went behind the counter, got a tray and put three mugs and a pot of coffee on it. He carried the tray to the table, sat down and without asking poured them each a cup. Mike began to drink his. *How can anyone drink coffee at a time like this?* she wondered. Deni put a lot of milk in her mug. She tried not to make a face when she took a sip of the liquid. She hated coffee.

Mr. Larson methodically lit his pipe, then inhaled thoughtfully. The sweet odor of pipe tobacco swirled around them. "Couldn't have been Presbyterian or Lutheran, and you said you knew it wasn't Reverend Schmidt at the Methodist church," he said at last. "But maybe Congregational."

"That's what the librarian thought!" Deni said eagerly.

"There was a Reverend Powell here in the late 1960s, as I recall. Had three daughters. You said you were wanting to find him?"

"Actually, it's one of the daughters. The one we want to find would have been eighteen in 1969." Deni held her breath, her hands in tight fists in her lap. So far Mike hadn't said anything at all, but she was glad he was there.

Mr. Larson stroked his chin. "That would have been Elaine, I reckon. I remember Elaine. A nice girl, in fact, a real nice family. But—"

"But what?" Mike asked. She glanced at him, pleased. He was getting involved.

"Well, they were kind of different. Not real small town folks, I reckon. People didn't know them real well," he said.

Mr. Larson, were there ever any—rumors about Elaine?" Deni asked. She tried to keep her voice even as she asked this. Her hands were starting to shake again, so she kept them under the table.

He chuckled. "Folks always love to gossip, that's part of human nature. I don't suppose there was ever any more gossip about her or her sisters than about most young people. Usually there's nothing to any of it."

She tried another tactic. "Did—Elaine—work in Topeka after high school? Possibly as a nurse's aide? You see, we know that the girl we're looking for did, and—"

"I don't remember where she worked," he

173

interrupted. "The family moved away from here in the early seventies. Went south somewhere."

"But Elaine—did she—" Deni faltered.

"Were there ever rumors that Elaine had a baby out of wedlock?" Mike cut in, his voice steady. Deni shot him a grateful look. "That's what we really want to know, Mr. Larson."

"Why?"

Deni glanced quickly at Mike.

"It's important. A family matter," Mike said. His voice was forceful, and he looked Mr. Larson directly in the eye, something Deni hadn't been able to do.

Mr. Larson puffed on his pipe and looked out the front windows. "Well, can't say that ever happened. I don't think anyone here would know about that. But it's possible there were some rumors."

Mike and Deni exchanged glances. Mr. Larson seemed to know more than he was willing to tell them. Deni caught the old man looking hard at Mike and her. *He knows,* she thought to herself. *He knows why we're asking.* She looked directly at him. "Mr. Larson, do you know where she—where *Elaine*—might live?"

Mr. Larson looked at her quizzically and took a long draw on his pipe. "Well, it's a funny thing," he said slowly. "She's the one who stayed in the area. The rest of them left."

Deni's heart seemed to jump to her throat, and her right hand gripped the handle of her coffee mug. She took a deep breath, trying to keep her voice controlled. "Where is she?" she asked, her voice almost a whisper.

"Baldwin," he replied calmly, his steady gaze on her. "A little town about, oh, twenty miles southwest of here. Married a nice boy there, from what I heard, a mechanic." He carefully relit his pipe, taking another long draw on it. "Kind of an odd name, if I recall. Brommer? Bremer? Something like that. And you know what, missy?" He grinned at Deni, his eyes twinkling. "I think Elaine probably is that long-lost cousin you're looking for. I remember her. And you and her got the very same eyes."

Chapter Fourteen

The map lay open on Deni's lap. She gazed out the car window. Even without looking at Mike she knew the expression on his face. She had seen it before.

He had stopped the car at the edge of town within view of the highway. They were at an impasse. Mike wanted to return to Topeka, Deni wanted to drive to Baldwin.

Whey they had come out of the café, the sun was shining, heating the soaked earth and making everything steamy and moist. The headache she felt the first twinges of an hour before was building, intensified by the humidity and the tension growing between her and Mike. She wished she had some aspirin and a glass of cold—very cold—water.

"It looks on the map like Baldwin is about twenty miles from here, just like Mr. Larson said," she ventured to say, trying to keep her voice pleasant. "And the highway is paved the whole way. We have time. Nobody is expecting us back in Topeka before five o'clock."

"That's not the point," he said, his voice tight.

"I know the point. It's because of my mom. You figure I'm going to hurt my mother."

"I *know* you're going to hurt her," he retorted.

She bit her lip. When she spoke, her voice was tense, angry. "Look, Mike, don't I have some rights, too? Why did anybody have the right to give me away in the first place? And why did somebody else have the right to take me? What about *me*? Don't I have a right to know who I am?" Tears stung her eyes. Deni kept her voice low, but it was trembling with emotion. "Nobody ever thinks about adoptees," she said. "Don't you think these two 'mothers' of mine owe me a few things, too? One person gives a baby up to another person. The baby can't say anything about that. Well, this baby has grown up, and I have a right to know some things now, things nobody else had a right to keep from me."

"I don't think you have any idea why you're doing this or what these 'things' are," he said sharply. "One minute you're searching for this rich, beautiful fantasy creature who will give you a wonderful life. Then you're searching for your future best friend, or you're looking for genetic information about blood relatives. But what I think you're really planning is to confront her just to give yourself some sort of satisfaction. Maybe once she sees you and how 'nicely' you've turned out, she'll regret that she put you up for adoption." Mike's eyes flashed. "Is that it, Deni? Is revenge the driving force here?"

"It's none of your business!" she cried. "Why did you come if this is how you're going to act? What right do you have to question my motives? You can't understand because you're not adopted."

"Deni," he said, "you can't just show up on Elaine's doorstep. It's not fair to her, assuming that this Elaine is even the right person. Whatever 'evidence' we have right now is pure speculation. We don't have *any* facts. But even if she *is* the right person and even if everything goes fine and she's glad to see you, I don't think your motives are clear enough to prevent you from getting hurt. Has it occurred to you that *all three* of you—both of your mothers and you—could end up losers?"

Deni was crying now, and her head throbbed. She turned toward him, her eyes filled with tears. "How can I explain to you what it's like having nobody in the world you can connect to, someone you're biologically related to?" she asked him. "I feel so alone, Mike. I have a loving family, I've been lucky. I had a wonderful grandmother, I have a new nephew I couldn't love more. But don't you see? I *need* to know that there's someone else on the face of this earth that I'm a part of. I just want to see her and know she's there. You saw Mr. Larson. He *knew*. It's Elaine. And I *will see her*."

She shifted her body away from him and stared out at the soggy baseball diamond they had parked beside. She heard him pound the steering wheel with his hands, twist in his seat, and then slump down. "OK," he muttered. "OK. If I don't go with you today, you'll just go on your own tomorrow. Let's get it over with. You win."

To Deni, her victory felt a little empty. She couldn't make him understand.

They said very little during the drive to Baldwin. Deni wanted to tell Mike how glad she was that he was with her and that she didn't want to do it alone—not that day, or the next, or ever. But she couldn't say that now. For now she simply had to be content that he was with her and would be with her, no matter what happened.

At the edge of Baldwin, Mike pulled into a filling station. There were puddles everywhere. The sun beat down intensely when it peeked through the clouds, and the air was heavy, hot, and foreboding. To the west, dark storm clouds churned and rolled in the sky. Deni's headache was a persistent dull throb that made her eyes ache.

She rolled down the window and pretended to study the map as she listened to Mike talk to the station attendant. He mentioned "Brommer," "Elaine," and "mechanic."

Deni saw the attendant's face light up. "Sure," he said. "I know who you want. Ed and Elaine Brettmeyer. Only folks in Baldwin with that name. Ed's a good mechanic. Real trustworthy. They're nice folks. Religious."

Of course they're religious, Deni thought. *Her father is a minister.*

The attendant told Mike how to find the house. "I'm not sure which side of the road it's on," he said, "but their house is set as far as you can go on that street, so if it's not on one side, it's on the other."

When Mike got into the car, he smiled at Deni and reached for her hand, giving it a squeeze. "We're close," he said.

She smiled back, grateful that the tension between them had dissolved. Her thoughts were fuzzy. Did she look all right? Should she put on lipstick? Comb her hair? What should she do? Shake hands? Give Elaine a hug? What if her husband opened the door? Or perhaps she had other children? Deni felt a growing sense of panic. What was she going to say?

The last house on the road was a simple, square, two-story frame structure set back from a gravel road on the edge of town. Mike pulled up to the mailbox so Deni could read it. *Brettmeyer.* Deni nodded at Mike, and he pulled into the muddy drive. Then he turned off the engine. Deni was numb. How could her birth mother live there? She had given up the fantasy that her birth mother was rich and famous, but she hadn't expected to find her in something quite so humble and ordinary, something so typically *Kansas.*

Mike voiced her thoughts. "Remember, her husband is a mechanic, Deni."

She struggled with her feelings as she looked at the house. It needed paint but was otherwise in good repair. Flowers filled two large pots on the porch. A boy's BMX dirt bike leaned against a tree, and a girl's bike with pink streamers on the handlebars lay in the yard. Deni winched when she saw them.

"Now what?"

She took a deep breath. "Let's go find her."

"No. I'm staying here. You have to do this. Just remember that you may not have the right person, or she might not be home. And if the kids or her husband are around, don't say anything." He looked at her, frowning. "What *will* you say?"

Deni stared at the house. "I don't know."

"Let's go home." He made a motion to start the car.

"No. I can't. Just give me a minute to get myself ready." She rubbed her eyes and her temples, trying to think clearly. There was no plan. She had to play it by ear.

Deni drew in a deep breath, gave Mike a slight smile, and got out of the car. They were parked in mud, and she carefully stepped through it, her eyes on the ground. She was nervous and self-conscious. How many pairs of eyes were watching her? There was no sidewalk. She dodged puddles walking through the wet grass to the front door.

She rang the bell. There was no response.

She rang it again, but no one answered. Maybe nobody was home. Maybe it wasn't the right house. Maybe they had moved away. That thought was almost comforting. She rang the bell once more. Deni finally turned to Mike and shrugged. He was pointing, motioning to her to go around to the side of the house toward the car. He must have seen somebody there.

Walking through the grass, Deni kept her eyes down, avoiding patches of mud and water. The sun was still out, and its brightness hurt her eyes and intensified her headache. The air was heavy with humidity and was ominously quiet. Black clouds raced through the sky above her, about to shadow the sun.

As she turned the corner of the house, she saw a woman working in a garden. She was in full view of the car. She wore a sun dress and had light brown hair.

The woman glanced up. "Can I help you?" she asked. Her voice was wary, defensive.

Deni squinted, trying to see the woman in sunlight, searching for some familiar feature. She must be a neighbor, she couldn't be her mother.

"I said, can I help you?" The woman stood up, unsmiling. She was slim and fragile looking.

"I'm—looking for a woman named Elaine Brettmeyer," Deni said hesitantly. As she spoke, the sun went behind the clouds. Deni stared hard at the woman and felt her heart begin to pound as she gazed into dark brown eyes like the ones she saw in her own mirror every morning.

The woman looked at her guardedly. "You found her," she said, her voice flat. "I'm Elaine."

Chapter Fifteen

For an instant, one of the old fantasies flashed through Deni's mind: she and her birth mother—her beautiful, elegant, smiling mother—were strolling down Fifth Avenue in New York City, their arms linked, laughing and happy together.

In front of her stood a plain, hard-working, tired-looking woman who had dark brown eyes.

Elaine looked at her suspiciously. "Are you selling something? Didn't you see the sign on the door? No solicitors allowed."

Thunder suddenly boomed above them, startling Deni. The air was heavy, sticky, and still.

"I'm—could it be that—" Deni's knees felt weak. Her head was pounding. She needed to sit down. She felt a large raindrop plop onto her arm, then another. She tried again, her throat straining against the words. Her heart thumped so hard against her chest that it felt like it would burst. In a rush she blurted out, "Could it be that I'm your daughter?"

Elaine stared at her, shock on her face. In Deni's fantasy, there had always been instant, wordless recognition between mother and daughter, followed by a long, loving embrace and happy tears of joy.

It began to rain, the air suddenly cool. Deni shivered and waited for the woman to answer her.

"What are you talking about?" Elaine finally said, her voice almost a whisper. "Why are you asking me that?" She didn't seem to notice the rain, which was quickly becoming a downpour. Above them, thunder boomed like a drum roll and lightning cracked violently against the black clouds.

Deni took a step forward, but the woman moved back. Deni stopped. "I'm—adopted. I came across some information about my—my birth mother that has led me to you."

Elaine stared at Deni, her dark eyes disbelieving. Her wet sun dress clung to her thin body, and her soaked hair hung limply against her face.

Deni wiped the rain from her eyes. She waited, but the woman said nothing. Thunder clapped again, closer this time, startling her. She wanted to go back to the car, back to Mike. She knew he was watching. She looked imploringly at Elaine. "If I've made a mistake, I apologize. I won't bother you. I'll leave now."

No response. Nothing. Finally she turned to go, tears burning her eyes as she began to walk away.

"Why have you come? Do you want to ruin my life a second time?" Elaine yelled over a crack of thunder.

Stunned, Deni whirled around and faced her. "Are you my mother?" she asked quickly. "I was born August 8, 1969, in Topeka, and I—"

Elaine began to run toward the back door of the house. She paused at the steps. "Go away!" she cried. "Don't do this to me. Go away, and never come back!" She disappeared through the back door.

Deni stared at the house, her mind reeling, tears trickling down her face. She had found her. That was her birth mother. But how could a woman respond to her own daughter like that? This wasn't the way it was supposed to have been. It was supposed to have been a joyful reunion. Elaine hadn't even asked Deni how she had found her, or what her name was, or where she lived.

By the time Deni got to the car, she was sobbing, angry, and dripping wet. Her legs and feet were spattered with mud. She took the tissue Mike offered her and wiped her eyes and blew her nose.

"That was her, right?"

She nodded as she began to rummage in her purse. He waited while she found a pen and scrap of paper and hurriedly wrote a note, then handed it to him, a set look on her face. She knew he had seen everything that had happened.

"'I don't want to hurt you,'" he read out loud. "'I just want to know some facts about myself. If you will answer a few questions I won't bother you again. Please call me at work at this number between eight-thirty and twelve noon tomorrow. Denise Lambert.'" She had scrawled her phone number across the bottom of page page.

"Is it OK?" she asked him anxiously. "It shouldn't sound like blackmail. I just want her to talk to me." Before he could reply, she started to open the car door. She would put the message inside the front screen of the house.

Mike grabbed her arm. "Deni, leave her alone," he implored her. "You already have her answer. She obviously doesn't want anything to do with you. She just made that clear. You've seen her—that's enough. That's what you said you wanted. Let's go. Don't torment her."

Deni glared at him defiantly. Quickly she got out of the car and ran to the front door. She put the note inside the screen where it would stay dry, then rang the bell. She was certain Elaine was watching her from inside the house. No one else seemed to be home.

The rain was coming down harder than ever when she slid into the car, breathless, tears rolling down her cheeks, her sobs choking her. Mike had already started the car, and he backed out of the driveway. He drove down the road until he came to a turnoff, then parked on the side of the road, leaving the engine running and the windshield wipers flapping.

Mike pulled Deni to him, and with his arms around her, held her as she sobbed, her breath coming in hard gasps. He pushed the hair from her eyes and kissed the top of her head. Gradually she stopped crying and began to relax against him. He was so warm and so comforting and so protective, and she loved him.

As he kissed her, she pressed her body to his, her love for him engulfing her. Finally they drew apart and sat quietly in the car for several minutes, listening to soft music on the radio as the rain beat down around them.

Mike began to stroke her hair, and she snuggled into the crook of his arm, her eyes closed. "Drop it now before you get hurt even more, Deni," he whispered, his voice tender.

She didn't respond.

"Don't talk to her, even if she agrees."

Her answer was to give him a slight smile and a quick kiss on his lips.

Mike sat up straight, shaking his head as he pulled the car onto the highway. "If she does agree to talk to you," he said, exasperation in his voice, "find out where you get your stubborn streak. If you use half of your determination in the future, Deni, I swear you'll move mountains."

Chapter Sixteen

Deni sat at her desk, the telephone planted firmly in front of her. She wanted it to ring; she wanted it to be Elaine. It was only 9:00 A.M., and she had work to do, but since arriving at the station a half hour earlier, Deni hadn't been able to get anything done.

Would Elaine call her? And if she did, then what? Deni wouldn't be able to ask her any questions—too many people were around. She hadn't been thinking about that the day before. She should have suggested something else, like meeting somewhere private to talk. If Elaine had children—and the bikes in her yard surely meant that she did—she might not be able to make a secret telephone call.

"Hi, honey. You sure look nice today," Roberta said. She had just come up to Deni's desk. "I swear I never met anyone who could look as good in any color they put on the way

191

you can. That pink blouse and skirt are real sharp."

Deni smiled at her. "Thanks, Roberta. How are the kids?"

"As long as the sun is out, the kids are fine. Weatherman's finally saying the rain is all over with. I can't believe how much we've had lately. The mosquitoes are going to be the size of horses this summer." She leaned over Deni's desk and looked closely at her necklace. "I like this. Are you managing to save anything at all out of your paycheck? You keep showing up with new stuff."

"As a matter of fact, I *haven't* managed to," Deni said and laughed. "I was kind of depressed last night, and Mom and I went out to the mall. You know how it goes—I saw this, decided to try it on, and the rest is history."

"You got a right to be depressed," Roberta said sympathetically. Some families get more than their share all at once. But, hey, I hear some good things about you, too. Keith told me yesterday in the studio that you and Mike Hogan have had a couple of dates. Anything serious going on?"

Deni laughed self-consciously. "It's too soon to tell. We've only been going out a couple of weeks, but—"

"Yeah?" Roberta grinned expectantly.

"Let's just say it's promising."

"He's a real cutie. If I was you, I'd be real interested. But somebody said he had a girlfriend."

"Well, sort of," Deni said, hedging. "They're—you know—not seeing much of each other right now. It's kind of hard to explain."

"OK, honey, whatever you say," Roberta said and laughed. "I can't imagine any guy choosing someone else over you. Can't say I know Mike or anything, but he looks like he'd be a lot of fun."

Deni smiled, recalling the long kiss in the car the day before when they were parked during the rain.

"Good luck with him, honey," Roberta said, winking. "You're two nice kids. Say, we've got a busy morning coming up. Several salespeople. Hope they don't get in your way out here. And the *Capitol-Journal* is sending a reporter in to talk to Mr. Robbins about our kids in the adoption series. The agency called a few minutes ago, and it looks like little Freddie's placement is going through. The boy we're doing this week, Jake, is so cute I wish I could take him home with me. No, no, forget I said that. I got more kids than I can handle now. But Jake won't have any problems getting a home. That leaves Crystal, and I guess somebody's interested in her, too. A single woman, I heard." Roberta started toward her office. "See you later, honey."

Deni glanced at her watch. It was only nine-fifteen. The phone had rung three times since eight-thirty, and each time her heart had leaped into her throat. If Elaine didn't call, Deni might have to go back to her house. But that might be too risky. No one else seemed to have been there yesterday, but she might not be so lucky the next time.

Deni folded her hands in her lap. She hoped that Mike would stop by her desk on his break. When he had dropped her off at home, he told her as gently as he could that he was going to see Heather that evening. He didn't say what they were going to do, and she hadn't asked. She wished she could see him and try to determine if anything was different about how he felt, but she wasn't about to leave her desk, not even for him.

The front doors opened, and an older woman came in with a young girl. The woman, who seemed unsure and self-conscious, smiled hesitantly at Deni. The little girl kept her eyes downcast. She looked very familiar.

"Hi!" Deni said brightly. "May I help you?"

"We just wanted to see the station," the woman said politely. She motioned to the little girl. "Crystal was on your news show last week and—"

"Crystal? Of course! I'm *so* pleased to meet you," Deni said, coming around the front of the desk. "I'm *honored!*"

The little girl looked at her, surprised, then ducked her head again. "I saw Crystal on your show, and we're spending the day together. I'm Ann Blake. I called last week and talked to a very nice person here—"

"Are you the college professor?" Deni asked. The woman nodded. "You talked to me. I'm Deni Lambert. Hope I didn't come on too strong with that sales pitch." She smiled at them both. "It's great that the two of you came to visit us. To really see the station, you'll have to come back for one of our regular tours, but there are a few things you can look at."

The little girl kept her eyes on her feet, her arms close to her sides. Deni remembered what Mike had said about their difficulty in filming Crystal—her uncooperativeness and her sensitivity because of her crippled arm. She seemed ill at ease.

"I wonder," Ann Blake asked, "if Crystal could stay here with you for a minute? I need to run back to the car and get my sweater. It's much cooler in here than I had expected."

"Sure!" Deni said. "You can sit right here beside me, Crystal." She moved a chair behind the desk so it was next to her own. The little girl shyly sat down. Deni noticed how carefully she tried to hide her crippled arm by keeping it close to her body and using her other arm to do everything.

"How old are you?" Deni asked after Ann Blake left.

"Eight."

"Ann Blake seems very nice. I like her, don't you?" Deni asked.

The child shrugged. Deni felt her heart go out to her. She couldn't imagine how it must feel to know she was being "checked out" by someone who was thinking of adopting her.

"I hope you get adopted," Deni said. "Adoption is very nice. I'm adopted."

Crystal looked at her in surprise. "You are?"

"Yes. But I was adopted when I was a baby so I don't remember *not* being adopted."

Crystal didn't respond.

"Maybe someday I'll adopt a child," Deni continued. "I think it's pretty special."

"No one wanted me," Crystal said.

Deni blinked. How could she help this child? Could there be any worse feeling than to think no one wanted you? "Well, I think you're a very beautiful girl," she said softly. "I'll bet lots of families would love to adopt you. The problem is usually with the adoption system. The way it works is pretty strange sometimes. What I mean is, it can take too long. I think you should have been adopted a long time ago."

"It's because of my arm," Crystal said, sitting very still on her chair. "I was born this way."

Deni had an overwhelming desire to hug Crystal to reassure her. How lucky Deni had been! She had never felt unwanted; her new family had loved her unconditionally.

Very gently, Deni touched the little girl's cheek. "That arm may give you some trouble, but everybody has things they don't like about themselves. We just have to learn to like ourselves the way we are. It's funny how it works, but if we like ourselves, then other people like us, too."

Crystal looked unconvinced.

"It's a fact," Deni went on. "If you just tried

to talk to people and ignored your arm, they would ignore it, too."

The girl was silent. Deni tried to think of something else to say to her. "When I said the adoption system is strange, what I meant was that it's hard sometimes to get the right children together with the right adults. That's why you were on TV. And it worked!" Deni said brightly. "Ann saw you and said to herself, 'There's a little girl who could use a mother. I could use a daughter. We should get together and see if we like each other.' "

"She *won't* like me," Crystal said.

"Why not?"

"You know," Crystal said. She motioned slightly to her crippled arm.

"Oh. You mean because you aren't perfect," Deni said.

"And I'm old."

"Maybe Ann isn't interested in a younger child. Maybe she's ready for a child who's old enough to do lots of things with her. Babies take an awful lot of care, you know," Deni told her.

"But my arm—" Crystal persisted.

"If Ann cared one bit about your arm, she wouldn't be here with you," Deni said, her voice reassuring.

The little girl sat quietly, staring down. The phone rang, startling Deni. Her heart sank when she discovered that it was a salesman confirming an appointment.

Ann Blake returned with her sweater and thanked Deni for watching Crystal. While Deni called the studio to arrange for the two of them to watch a show being taped, they went into the bathroom. Ann Blake came back alone. "Crystal will be right out," she said. "Isn't she a sweet child?"

"Oh, yes," said Deni enthusiastically. "She's a little shy, and she's self-conscious about her arm, but she'll get over that. She's a wonderful little girl."

"You sound like a matchmaker," Ann Blake said pleasantly. "Crystal told me in the bathroom that you're adopted. I guess that gives you a different perspective."

"Well, I know how important family is," Deni said.

"I've always wanted a child, but I'm not sure I can offer a good home. I'm financially secure, and I'd like to share my life with someone. With a *child*. But"—she hesitated—"maybe it wouldn't be fair to a child. After all, I'm just an old college professor, unmarried, and pretty set in my ways."

"But think of the security you can offer!" Deni said. "And you're settled. You've worked hard, and you're ready to take the time to really get to know a child and spend time with her."

Ann nodded. "My thoughts exactly. I guess adoption has made you very open to nontraditional families, hasn't it?"

"Sure!" Deni said. Crystal was coming out of the bathroom. Deni spoke hurriedly. "Will you let me know what happens?" she asked the woman. "Maybe if Crystal could talk to someone once in a while who had been adopt-ed—I mean me, of course—well, maybe that would help her."

"How nice of you to offer!" Ann Blake said, taking Crystal's hand. "Yes! I'll do that."

As they started toward the studio, the little girl glanced back shyly. Deni waved at her. Was there a glimmer of a smile on the child's face? She watched until the studio door closed behind them.

Chapter Seventeen

"Deni? Everything OK? You look worried about something."

Chuck stood on the other side of Deni's desk. She tried to give him a big smile. "Sorry," she said. "Just—little things." She glanced at the phone. "Everything's fine. Really."

Chuck looked skeptical. "Well, I wanted to stop and tell you that things are still going well with Kara and the baby. They both got through the night without any problems. Kara might go home tomorrow!"

"That's wonderful," Deni smiled. "John Christopher will be home before you know it. You only have to look at him to tell he's a fighter."

Chuck grinned happily. "He's great, isn't he? I was completely unprepared for how much I love him. Becoming a parent is so—I don't know—it's instantly overwhelming, and yet it's so wonderful. All of a sudden you feel such love for this little person you never knew before." He got a funny look on his face and gave her a crooked smile. "Sort of like when Mom and Dad and I adopted you. One day there you were, and we just opened right up and drew you in, and it was like the most natural thing in the world to have you as part of the family.

"You're embarrassing me, Chuck," Deni said and giggled. "I mean, I know I'm wonderful and all"—she gave him an impish smile—"but even wonderful little me has faults. I've given the family some hard times. Remember when I started collecting heavy metal rock albums? Mom was threatening to take my stereo away just to preserve her sanity!"

"Thanks for reminding me. Now that I think about it, you've become a real pain in the—"

"Same to you," she said, grinning.

"Is Mom sleeping better?" Chuck asked.

"I guess so," Deni answered. She felt a sharp stab of guilt. "I haven't been looking out for her as much as I should have."

"Well, we can only tell her so much, and we've both told her to take it easy. Her responses to problems are to eat a big breakfast, keep a stiff upper lip, and stay busy," Chuck said. "She bottles up her feelings and lets you think she's doing just fine. She was that way when Dad died. Remember?"

Deni nodded. "Everyone kept saying how well she was doing and the next thing we knew, she was having back spasms and ended up in bed on painkillers for two weeks."

"Just keep after her, Deni, and watch for signs of trouble. Give me a call if I can help. I'm relying on your judgment."

Surprised and pleased, Deni looked at her brother. "I will, Chuck. Without Gram here anymore, it's up to you and me to watch out for her."

"Don't kid yourself," he said. "She's looking out for us just as much as we look out for her. That's how family works."

The phone rang, startling her. Chuck gave her a curious look as she slowly and deliberately reached for it. If it was Elaine, how could she talk in front of him? When the voice at the other end asked for the time, she gave an audible sigh of relief. She looked at the clock. "It's five minutes after ten," she said and then hung up. "Sometimes I think I should tell people they've reached information instead of a TV station," she told Chuck.

Chuck laughed. "I always feel better when I'm around you, Deni. You always know how to handle things. Listen, when this is all over, when things have calmed down, we really are going out to lunch. Just you and me. We should spend more time together. I'd suggest today, but Mom is meeting me at the hospital to talk to me about something. She won't tell me what. I know she's looking for a realtor for Gram's house. I have a couple of people in mind. But about going out to lunch sometime—what do you say?"

Deni tried not to show how pleased she was. "I'll see if I can work it into my schedule. I'm *very* busy these days. If I don't have my paycheck spent within forty-eight hours of receiving it, I get depressed. You know how it is with us professional shoppers."

"Yes," he said. "And I've also noticed that you're spending quite a bit of time with one of our camera interns." He grinned.

"Can I help it if he's so crazy about me?" she asked him.

Chuck left then, and Deni hugged herself. He was really noticing, at long last, that she was growing up. And her mother was going to talk to him that noon about their grandmother's house! She could hardly wait to find out how Chuck reacted to the idea of him, Kara, and the baby living there. It was the perfect solution!

The morning dragged by despite her steady flow of work. Salespeople were in and out of the station, overflowing Mr. Robbins's waiting area and taking up the seating by her desk. The phone had rung all morning with requests ranging from schedule and weather information to tips on news stories and personal messages. There had been so many calls that Deni was afraid that Elaine might have tried to call and hadn't been able to get through.

By eleven-thirty she was anxious and irritable. Two salespeople, a man and a woman, were still waiting to see Mr. Robbins. They were seated near her desk, talking together and ignoring Deni.

Mike came up behind her and touched her hair with his fingertips as he plunked down on a corner of her desk. "Nice pink outfit," he said. "Goes good with that beautiful hair. Any special phone calls this morning?" He winked at her.

"No." Deni felt a rush of warmth flood her body. She wanted to kiss him. He was wearing his favorite pair of faded jeans and an old David Bowie T-shirt. "What do I do now?"

"It's not noon yet. You've got twenty minutes to go. As a famous baseball player once said, 'The game isn't over till it's over.' I saw Crystal."

"Did you get to talk to her?"

"Keith and I were doing some camera maintenance, so we invited her down into the studio and showed her the cameras. After you tried to help me see things from her point of view, I approached her differently this morning. Know what?" Mike asked. "She's kind of shy, but certainly not hostile. She's really a sweet little kid. I guess I acted like a real jerk that day we filmed her."

Deni patted his hand. "Don't be too hard on yourself. Your heart's in the right place. And speaking of hearts—"

"I know what's coming," he said. "You want to know how things went with Heather last night. I thought you weren't going to ask."

"You brought her up," Deni said. "Not me. But forget I said anything."

"That's OK. I was going to tell you anyway that we—" As Mike spoke, Deni saw the saleswoman seated near her get up from her chair. She looked pale and dizzy. Then she sat down hard, holding her hand on her stomach. The man next to her signaled frantically at Deni. She rushed over, with Mike following right behind her.

"What's wrong?" Deni asked.

"She says she's sick," the salesman replied, worried. "Can you take her to the ladies' room?"

"Sure. It's just over there," Deni said. They helped the woman to her feet. "Mike, can you stay for a minute and *answer* the phone?" She glanced at him. "If I get that call I'm waiting for, come get me." Mike nodded knowingly, and Deni guided the woman to the restroom.

When she returned a few minutes later, Mike was again sitting on the corner of the desk. The salesman was standing by him, and they were talking about cameras.

"How is she?" the salesman asked.

"She'll be fine. She says she's had the flu and thought she was over it. She's going to wash up and then leave. I already told Roberta to reschedule her. Any calls?" she asked Mike anxiously.

He shook his head and went back to talk to the salesman.

Deni stared at the phone. It was noon. Elaine hadn't called. She put the noon hour phone message on, locked the desk, and then looked expectantly at Mike. Maybe he would at least walk her to her car. She wanted to talk to him. Not only did she want to know about his date with Heather the night before, but now she had to try to figure out what to do about Elaine. She tried to get his attention. He and the salesman were busy comparing notes on wide angle lenses.

"Bye, Mike," she said. She waited for him to answer.

He waved at her. "I'll call you later," he said, his voice indifferent. He didn't look at her.

Hurt and angry, she glared at both of them and hurriedly left the station. How could Mike ignore her like that! He had to know how disappointed she was not to have heard from Elaine. He could have at least given her a chance to talk about it. She had to figure out what she was going to do.

How many options did she have? Deni *had* to talk to Elaine. She had questions she wanted answered. There were things she wanted to know. Only Elaine could tell her who her birth father was. Why hadn't she just called? Was that asking so much? Didn't Elaine owe her that?

As Deni reached her car, she saw Mike coming quickly toward her through the parking lot, his slim body slipping easily between the parked cars.

"Since Elaine didn't call, I guess you'll drop the whole thing now," he said, coming up to her. His voice sounded hopeful.

She glanced sharply at him, anger on her face. "No. I'll go back and see her again."

"That won't accomplish anything—"

"Maybe this time she'll listen."

"And maybe she won't," he said flatly. His voice sounded impersonal. He wouldn't look at her.

She was confused. He had been so loving and caring. She frowned at him. "Whose side are you on? I don't understand you, Mike. You've done so much to help me, but still you try to stop me."

"I'm trying to stop you from making a mistake," he said.

"Here we go again!" she exclaimed. "Mike, I've seen her now. She knows I exist and that I'm here and that I want to talk to her. She owes me some answers."

His voice was firm, unyielding. "She owes you nothing. She gave you life. You have no right to ask for anything more."

"I want to know who my father is! I have a right to know that!" She glared at him. "Elaine and whoever he is are my family. That has to mean something!"

Deni was surprised to hear so much anger in Mike's voice. "Flesh and blood aren't the ingredients that make people family," he said, his words spilling out. "That's something that comes with living together and loving each other. You know I'm on your side, but the way I see it, you've already lost."

She started to protest, but he stopped her. "Your biological parent—and that's all Elaine is—has fallen far short of your expectations. You had disappointment written all over your face yesterday. And Elaine—think what this does to her to have you show up. Giving birth to a baby at the age of eighteen couldn't have been the greatest experience of her life. Now she's married, she has kids, and suddenly there you are, wanting to be part of her life. But you *aren't* part of her life. You're part of her *past* life only."

Deni wanted to run away from him. Why was he doing this to her? What right did he have to say all this?

"Elaine thought she had closed the door to the past," he said, moving closer to her. "Think what painful memories you open up for her. Think how this could affect the life she's built with her family."

Mike paused. "And then there's your mom. She has more to lose than anybody. Last week she lost her mother. This week it might be the love and loyalty of her only daughter. You're so ready to go off and be best friends with this 'new' mother. Why don't you think about the other people who could get hurt by what you're doing instead of being so blind, stupid, and selfish?"

"What?" Deni said incredulously, her voice rising. "If the shoe was on the other foot, you can bet it would be a different story. What do you think it feels 'like to wonder why your birth mother gave you away—and to not even know who your father was? All my life I've wondered why I was given up by my own mother. Was I so ugly? So awful? If she was poor, couldn't we have gotten along somehow? And doesn't she ever wonder about me and how I'm doing? And what about *him*? Who is he? *Where* is he?

"Don't you see, Mike? I'll say it again: *I want to be connected to someone*," she said, her voice breaking. "You've always had that, and I have a right to that, too. If that's selfish, then I'm selfish. But I have to do this for me. I thought you understood." She unlocked her car door and then looked back at him. Her voice was barely a whisper. "I want to feel *normal*. Like other people. Like you. I never have before. This is my chance, and I can't give it up."

"Geez, Deni—some burden!" Mike said, his voice full of irritation. "You act like you're the only person in the world who ever had a problem. Why don't you think about all the good things in your life instead? Why aren't you grateful that some good people adopted you and raised you? Why can't you just accept things the way they are and get on with it?"

She had to get away from him. She would not cry in front of him. Hastily she slid into the driver's seat and slammed the door. The car was hot, and she rolled down the window. She started the engine and gunned it.

"Deni, wait—" He grabbed her arm through the window and held it tight when she tried to pull away. Then, with his other hand, he dropped a pink phone slip on her lap and let go of her arm. She stared straight ahead. "I came out here to give you that message in private," he said. "I was also hoping to talk you out of going much further with this. She called while you were in the restroom." Mike paused, waiting, but she continued to stare straight ahead, the pink phone message still on her lap. He sighed and stepped back from the car. "The smartest thing you could do would be to call her and cancel," he said at last. "It's time to bury the past and live in the present."

"Go away," Deni said. "Just leave me alone from now on. I don't want to see you again. *Ever.*"

She refused to look at him. He'd had no right to say those things to her or to try to make her change her mind before giving her the message. He had *no right!*

As he walked away, the tears rolled unchecked down her cheeks. She was better off without him. He didn't understand her at all!

Deni picked up the pink slip of paper. Slowly she unfolded it. In Mike's handwriting, next to "Message From" he had written "Elaine." Under "Message" he had written "Will meet you at Dunkin' Donut shop on Twenty-third Street in Lawrence. Half hour only. 3:00 P.M. today."

Chapter Eighteen

The three o'clock news had just come on the radio when Deni drove into the parking lot at the doughnut shop. She parked on the side of the building and put her car keys in her purse. *This is it,* she said to herself. *This is my chance to get to know my birth mother.* Curiously, she didn't feel nearly the surge of excitement she had thought she would. What was wrong?

Maybe it was Elaine's attitude that was wrong. Where was the joy, the thrill of being reunited with her birth daughter? Why had she acted so defensive? No one could blame her for being surprised—Deni had simply stepped back into her life after almost seventeen years. But it would be all right. Once the ice was broken, they would become friends. It wasn't going to be as easy as Deni had imagined it would be, but it would work out.

It was a hot afternoon, and Deni knew it

would be cool inside the shop, but she lingered in the car, wondering if Elaine was in there yet. As Deni got out of the car, she smoothed the skirt of her yellow dress. Deciding what to wear had been extremely difficult. She had finally put on her light yellow oxford-cloth dress, confident—or at least until now she had been confident—that she looked her best in it. She glanced in the rearview mirror. Her dark brown hair was shiny and neat. She had pulled it back from her face with small gold barrettes. But her eyes looked tired and anxious. Well, she couldn't do anything about that now.

For a moment, Deni thought of Mike, pleading with her to cancel the meeting. Tears stung her eyes. Mike was wrong. She couldn't stand his criticism, and she wasn't going to listen to it ever again. Her relationship with him was over—Heather could have him.

She took a deep breath, then slowly walked into the doughnut shop. Was Elaine watching her? But she saw with a quick glance that Elaine wasn't there yet.

She was dismayed at the setting. The shop was too small, too well lit. It was not a good place for the kind of meeting that Deni had envisioned. Why had her mother—why had *Elaine*—picked it? Because it was the edge of town toward Baldwin? Because it was easy to find? Several people sat at the counter and two others at the closely spaced tables along the front windows. Private conversation would be difficult. *Maybe that's why Elaine picked it*, Deni thought.

A plump redheaded teenager stood behind the counter. "Miss, do you want something?" she asked.

Deni forced herself to survey the display case in front of her. She was too nervous to eat anything.

"Miss?" The clerk's voice was edgy with impatience. Deni hesitated. Out of the corner of her eye she saw a car pull into a parking place by the door. Deni turned to look at it and saw Elaine in the driver's seat. The car was a large sedan, old and nondescript.

Deni's heart began to pound in her chest. She looked back frantically at the clerk, who stared at her. "I'll take—two coffees. And two doughnuts."

"*Two* coffees? To go or for here?"

"Two," she said to the clerk. "For here." Perhaps if she drank coffee, much as she hated it, Elaine would view her as more adult and might take her more seriously. Little touches were important.

"What kind of doughnuts?" the clerk asked.

"What?" Deni asked.

"I said, what kind of doughnuts do you want? You just said two doughnuts. What kind?"

Deni was unable to do more than glance at the rolls, doughnuts, and cookies arranged before her in neat trays. "Anything," Deni said. She turned and saw Elaine coming through the door. "Plain will be fine."

"Did you say plain?" The clerk was starting to sound hostile.

"Yes. Thanks." She paid for the coffee and doughnuts. Elaine was standing near her, looking around.

"Hi," Deni said, her voice trembling. Didn't Elaine recognize her?

Startled, Elaine looked at her. "Hello," she said. Her voice was flat and noncommittal. She did not smile.

"I ordered for us," Deni said, picking up the tray with the doughnuts and coffee on it. Elaine started to move toward one of the window tables, and Deni nervously followed her. Neither of them said anything as she put the tray down. She forced herself to smile at Elaine. Elaine kept her eyes down, then took a pack of cigarettes out of her purse and lit one. "I don't like coffee. I hope you don't mind," she said.

"I don't either," Deni said quickly. "I—I guess I'm just like you." She smiled slightly as she said this, but Elaine was looking out the window at the traffic.

The coffee and doughnuts sat untouched between them. For an instant Deni felt nauseous. She fought back the feeling, shifting uncomfortably on her chair. The silence was awkward. "What shall I call you?" she asked brightly. "I guess you know from my note that my name is Denise—but everyone calls me Deni."

"My name is Elaine."

"Well, yes, I know, but I wondered—"

"Just Elaine."

"OK," Deni said. She hesitated and cleared her throat. If only her heart would stop pounding! "Thanks for meeting me today. I really appreciate it. I'm sorry about startling you yesterday. I—"

"How did you find me?" she asked, cutting Deni off abruptly. Elaine's words were sharp and direct. She kept her eyes on the street outside the window. Deni studied her. She was not a beautiful woman. Pleasant looking, simply dressed in a cotton skirt and blouse, no makeup. Deni had hoped she would be beautiful.

Deni fidgeted with the coffee cup. "I found a letter my mother—my *adoptive* mother— wrote my grandmother telling about my adoption, and it said where you were from and that your father was a minister," Deni answered. She kept her voice low so no one would hear her, grateful that no one was seated next to them. "I went to Eudora and asked some questions. Don't worry," she added hastily when Elaine glanced at her, "No one knew why I was looking for you. I was very careful. Really."

"What do you want to know?" Elaine's voice was guarded. "You said you had questions."

"I want to know—about you," Deni said slowly.

Elaine took a deep drag on her cigarette, avoiding Deni's eyes. "I grew up a preacher's kid. We moved around a lot. I went to high school in Eudora." She paused, seeming to consider her next words. "My father expected my two sisters and me to be perfect, like my mother. They moved a long time ago, to Arkansas." She puffed on her cigarette. "What else?"

"Just things like—well, I like to draw. I thought maybe you did, too."

"Me?" She laughed shortly. It was the first time Deni had seen her smile. "No. But my sister does. She likes to draw birds. Anything else?"

Deni nodded. "I thought maybe you'd—I mean, do you—want to know anything about me?" she asked hopefully, her voice hesitant.

Elaine looked surprised.

"I just thought that maybe you'd like to know—that I'm OK," Deni said hurriedly. "I have a nice mother, and a brother, and I also have a new nephew. My father—my *adoptive* father—died in an automobile accident."

"That's too bad. I bet that was tough," Elaine said sympathetically.

"It was. He was a great dad," Deni told her. She paused. "I want to be an artist. I draw all the time. And I want to go to college."

Elaine stared out the window. Deni took a sip of her coffee, hoping it would push down the lump rising in her throat. Her hands were still shaking. It was incredible that she was sitting there talking to her birth mother! It was a fantasy come true, and yet it didn't seem like one. It was so much harder than she ever thought it would be. Her emotions tangled, she looked at Elaine. Elaine kept her eyes focused on some distant point. "Do you have an—occupation?" Deni asked.

"You mean a job? I'm a housewife. I got three kids. I like to garden."

"Oh." Deni tried to think. What were the questions she wanted to ask? "Sometimes I worry that maybe there's some inherited illness in the family or something—"

Elaine met her eyes for a moment, then looked away. "No. Nothing I know of, on either side. Don't worry about that. I filled out the medical form for the adoption file." She shifted uncomfortably in her chair, as though she knew what was coming. Deni waited, struggling to get her voice under control. The unspoken words hung between them. Finally, her voice almost a whisper, she asked, "Who is my father?"

For a moment she thought Elaine hadn't heard her. She sat very rigidly, puffing on her cigarette, staring at her hands. Deni waited, her own hands wrapped around her coffee cup. She had thought so little about her birth father that no childish fantasies could be destroyed in learning his identity. She was ready for anything.

"You won't be able to find him," Elaine said at last.

Deni stared at her, uncomprehending. "Why not?"

"I don't know where he is. He could be anywhere in the world, for all I know."

"Who is—"

"Just give me a minute. I'll tell you." She

took a final puff on her cigarette and ground it out, then immediately lighted another one, her hands shaking. "This isn't easy," she said, almost to herself.

Deni started to respond, but Elaine silenced her with a wave of her hand. She stared into her coffee cup and sighed heavily. "I met him in Topeka. After I graduated from high school, I didn't have anything to do. My father wanted me to go to college, but I wouldn't. I hated school. He was angry. Without telling me he enrolled me in this course in Topeka at a hospital, to learn to be a nurse's aide. I hated that more than school. I was lonely. I was living in this rooming house and I didn't have any friends. Then I met this guy, and he was nice to me."

"My father."

"Yeah. All I wanted was to get married and have kids. I'd never had a real boyfriend before. He said he liked me, and I thought maybe he'd marry me. So I—well, you know." She fell silent.

Deni's head was buzzing. "Where did he come from?"

"Tulsa. But his family moved around a lot, just like mine did. He worked in Topeka at one of the big packing plants. I forget which one. When I signed the adoption papers, I put on that form they give you everything I knew about him, even his name." She struggled, searching the past for the right words. "He was big, tall, and he had brown hair. When he found out I was pregnant—"

"He left," Deni said, finishing the statement for her. *And that was that,* she thought.

"Yes. He left," Elaine repeated. She took a long drag on her cigarette. "I hoped he'd marry me, but I didn't tell him I was pregnant until I started looking it. I probably knew he'd take off. The only thing he said was, 'It's not mine. Good luck, I'm going as far away as I can go.' I still remember that real clearly, that part about 'it's not mine.' " She looked at Deni. "I don't think I'd try to find him if I were you. He probably wouldn't give you the time of day. You don't look like him at all except for the color of your hair."

Deni suddenly felt very tired. She watched the cars outside the window flowing along Twenty-third Street. "My folkd stopped by to see me right after they guessed the truth," Elaine continued. "They made the arrangements for me to go into a home until you were born. It broke my mother's heart. Both my folks were real ashamed. And raising you myself was never even considered."

"We would have done all right," Deni whispered, her eyes filled with tears. "At least we would have been together. We would have found a way."

"Look. You have to understand this," Elaine said impatiently. "I had no skills, no way of supporting either of us. I wanted to get married, and this was seventeen years ago. Things were different than they are today. It was a disgrace to be an unwed mother. Who would have married me? And it would have ruined

221

my father. He's a *minister*, in a small church. The congregation wouldn't have tolerated it."

"Did you consider—not having me at all?" Deni asked suddenly, looking down. She felt Elaine's eyes on her and met them with her own. Elaine quickly looked away.

"No," she said quietly. "I didn't think like that."

"Oh." A tear fell on Deni's hand. She blinked others back. "Then couldn't you have found *some* way to keep me?"

"I needed my family," Elaine said pleadingly. "My sisters and my mother, especially. If I had kept you, my father never would have spoken to me again. I wasn't strong enough to keep you."

She ground out her half-finished cigarette and pulled out a new one. "They told me at the agency that you would go to a good home. They said they had lots of people waiting, and that you would make someone happy." She sounded angry. "They said *this* would never happen. The records would be sealed, and I could start a new life," she added.

They sat in silence for several long moments. Deni blew her nose and wiped her eyes. Elaine continued to smoke, staring out the window. Finally Deni said, "So you got married."

Elaine nodded. "I finished the nurse's aide class after you were born, and I got a job at the hospital in Baldwin. I met Ed at church." She looked at Deni. "He doesn't know anything about you. It would kill him to know.

We got kids. We're happy with each other," she said. "My folks never talk about what happened, and we didn't think people in Eudora ever knew. I can deny any rumors as long as you don't show up in my life. You know that, don't you? You could ruin me, you could ruin everything I have."

Deni kept her head down, the tears rolling down her cheeks. She couldn't answer.

"Look. I know this is hard for you. I understand that you had to wonder about me. I'm sorry it can't be different. But it can't." Elaine spoke rapidly. "I've given you everything I can give. That whole period of time was awful for me. My boyfriend deserted me and my family— you were much better off with your other folks. I can't do anything else for you," she said. "And you've got to promise you won't ever come around again."

Deni met her eyes again, eyes that matched hers perfectly. "Do you think maybe someday we—"

"No. Promise me you won't try to see me again. Please," Elaine said.

For a moment Deni didn't move. Then she slowly nodded. Elaine got up to leave. "You're a pretty girl. I can tell you've been raised well. I'm really happy to see that."

When Elaine stood up, Deni panicked. She slipped out of her seat and awkwardly moved toward her. Deni threw her arms around her. Elaine stiffened but did not draw back. Deni closed her eyes, tears spilling down her cheeks. Elaine gave her a quick embrace, and Deni

223

felt her brush her lips across her forehead.
Then Elaine drew away and walked rapidly
out the door.

Deni watched Elaine back her car out of
the parking spot and drive away. "Goodbye,"
she whispered. A smile lingered on her face.
Her birth mother had touched her—had actually kissed her—and somehow, after almost seventeen years, that was enough.

Chapter Nineteen

Deni sipped the cold, bitter-tasting coffee, trying to steel herself for the drive back to Topeka. It would take time to sort through what had happened. She was surprised to find that she felt strangely content, although she had one very real regret.

I shouldn't have surprised her like that, she said to herself. *I shouldn't have just shown up.* She knew she should have found someone to contact Elaine first and find out if she would see Deni. *What I did was unfair.*

Mike had tried to tell her that, but she wouldn't listen. She had considered only what *she* wanted. It hadn't occurred to her that Elaine had done what was best for them both by giving her up for adoption.

Her vision blurred as tears filled her eyes. Mike had seen everything so much more clearly than she had. But then, he had a different perspective—an outsider's perspective. Why hadn't he been able to understand that the search was simply something she had to do? If he could have understood her *need* to find her birth parent, then she could have understood his objection to how she had gone about it.

Not that it mattered now. Meeting her birth mother had relieved Deni of a real burden. But in the process of freeing herself from the past, she had lost Mike.

Finally she left the doughnut shop, trying to adjust her eyes to the blinding sunlight as she walked to her car.

It wasn't until she reached it that she noticed Mike standing right next to it.

"Hi," he said casually, a grin on his face. "I just happened to get hungry for doughnuts and thought I'd drive to Lawrence for some. You recommend the ones here?"

They embraced without a word.

"Are you ready to talk?" Mike asked Deni. She was sitting in his car. They had left hers at the doughnut shop.

She smiled at him. "It's so pretty here. I can tell you're going to like going to college here if you're never more than a minute or two away from such a beautiful little lake."

"Let's walk down to the water," he said.

They got out of his car and started down the hill to Potter's Lake on the University of Kansas campus.

"You think my car will be OK where I left it?"

"Sure. We won't be here long." Mike took Deni's hand and gently squeezed it. "I just thought maybe you could use a little time to—"

"I'm sorry, Mike," she interrupted. "I acted so stupid this morning—"

"No, *I'm* sorry. I was too hard on you."

"Truce?" She smiled.

"Truce. Let's just say we both did some things we regret," he told her.

"Agreed." They found a shady spot near the water and sat down. She kicked off her shoes, relishing the feel of the cool grass against her feet. "I won't be seeing her again," she said.

"I didn't figure you would. I watched her leave. She never looked back."

"But I'm still glad I found her."

"Why?"

Deni hesitated. "I don't quite understand it yet, but somehow I'm satisfied just to have seen her and to have gotten to know her a little bit. She's not at all what I had imagined. She's just a very ordinary person who solved a problem the way that was best for her—and for me," she added. "I don't think it would have been much of a life for us together. I think she would have been pretty bitter."

Mike lay on his side, his head propped on his elbow. "If you had it to do over again, would you change anything?"

She looked at him. His eyes were twinkling, and he had a bemused look on his face. "I would," she said seriously. "I don't regret that I searched for her or that I found her."

"But?" he asked.

"I shouldn't have just shown up on her doorstep like that. You tried to tell me that. I could have had someone else contact her first."

"What if she hadn't agreed to see you?" Mike asked.

Deni thought for a moment. "The only fair thing would have been to accept that. But I think she would have seen me. She said she could understand my curiosity. As it was, she *had* to talk to me because I was such a threat to her, and that didn't get us off to a good start," Deni conceded.

Mike tickled her toes with a long stem of grass. "So you do feel better now?"

"Yes. At least I won't be searching the faces of strangers any more, trying to find someone who looks like me. And I can unload a lot of years worth of fantasies about who she is," Deni told him.

She told Mike what she had learned about her birth father. "I don't have enough to go on to try to find him, and I don't think I'd want to anyway. It doesn't matter anymore. I can feel normal now. And that feels great." She smiled at him. "What else do you want to know?" she asked him.

"What about telling your mom?"

"Maybe someday. Not now. I think I can understand why she's never been able to be open with me about my adoption. She just doesn't like to be reminded that I'm not her own child. Mike," Deni said, "what I think I realized this afternoon is that my mother and my brother and I really *are* family, that we became a family the moment I was adopted. Chuck said John Christopher's birth showed him how much we're capable of opening up and loving others. And he and my folks opened up like that when they brought me home. I immediately became family. My mother is probably afraid that if I found my birth mother, it would hurt my relationship with her."

Mike looked at her intently. "Has it?"

"No. Isn't that strange?" Deni said wonderingly. "If anything, I love her more. I realize now what a terrific mother she's been. Elaine is my biological parent, but that's all. She's my 'other' mother. My mom raised me, and she's my real mom."

Mike laid his head down in her lap and smiled up at her. "How did you manage to make everything turn out all right?" he asked.

"Easy," she said flippantly and kissed the tip of his nose. "I listened to everything *you* said and then did just the opposite." Mike laughed and pulled her down to him for a long-awaited kiss.

When Deni turned her car into the driveway an hour later, her mother rushed out the front door to meet her. She waved at Mike as he pulled in behind Deni in his Honda.

"The baby is going home!" she cried, hugging Deni as she stepped out of the car.

"Chuck called just a few minutes ago, and everything's going so well that John Christopher will go home tomorrow with Kara!"

Deni yelped in delight, excitedly telling Mike the news as he walked over to them.

"To celebrate, Chuck wants to take us all out to dinner tonight, six-thirty," Mrs. Lambert said smiling. "You're invited, too, Mike. Can you come?"

Deni looked at him expectantly.

"I wouldn't miss it." He grinned. "Why don't I pick up the two of you at six-fifteen?"

"That would be lovely," Mrs. Lambert said.

"I like him, Deni," she commented a few minutes later as Mike drove away. "He seems levelheaded. And sincere. Smart and sincere."

"Not only that," Deni said, putting her arm around her mother's waist, "he's truthful— even when you don't want to hear it. At times that can be a pain in the neck, but overall I'd say it's in his favor."

Her mother looked searchingly at her. "I know how hard the last few weeks have been for you, Deni. I've noticed several times that you've looked troubled, but because of my own problems, I haven't made much effort to see if I could help. I hope you know that I'm always here if you need me."

"Sure, Mom," Deni said, "I know that. But I've got everything worked out. Just so *you're* OK."

They sat down at the kitchen table, and Deni sipped the glass of lemonade her mother poured for her. "I'm getting there," her mother said. "The news about Kara and the baby are the best medicine possible. My mother's death and John Christopher's birth have made me realize more than ever how precious family is to us. I hope I don't forget that."

"I've learned a few things myself," Deni agreed.

Her mother gave her a questioning look. "Like what?"

"Well," Deni said thoughtfully, "there are good secrets, and there are bad ones. All of us, sooner or later, keep secrets from one another if we think it's in their best interest. Maybe someday I'll tell you one of my secrets," she said and laughed mysteriously. "But right now," Deni said, finishing her lemonade, "I'm going to get dressed for dinner and put the finishing touches on a sailboat drawing."

Late that evening as Deni and Mike approached her front door from their after-dinner walk, Deni said suddenly, "Just wait right there! I have something for you."

He sat down on the porch steps, and a moment later she came back, a small, flat, wrapped package in her hands. "For you," she said simply, smiling at him.

He opened it slowly, a look of pleasure spreading across his face. "It's the sailboat you were sketching at the lake! It's great, Deni. You got that sail just perfect," he said.

"I'm glad you like it," she said, pleased. She sat down next to him. "It's a thank-you gift for the picture of me you gave my mom.

She likes it so much she really is going to get it framed and put it on the mantel. Actually," Deni added, "it's not a thank-you gift. I was planning to give it to you all along."

"I'll take it to school with me this fall and hang it in my room," Mike said. "Maybe it'll help me study when the going gets rough. It'll remind me that I need to graduate and get a good job so I can buy my own sailboat!"

He kissed her tenderly, and she snuggled close to him.

"I'm so happy that Chuck and Kara are going to move into my grandmother's house," Deni said after a moment. She giggled. "But the look on my mom's face when Chuck said he wanted to put solar collectors on the roof and skylights over the kitchen was funny! She had trouble picturing that!"

"Deni—" Mike said abruptly.

"Hmmm?"

"I saw Heather last night."

Deni felt a sudden surge of fear go through her body. "You told me you were going to," she said cautiously.

"We had a long talk," he said. "And we decided not to see each other anymore. It's all over."

"That's—good," Deni said after a moment, trying not to show her delight. "I hope you'll be happy with that decision."

They sat quietly for several moments, enjoying the cool night air, the moon full above them. "Are you pleased that Chuck asked you to work at the station over Christmas vacation?" she finally asked. She would ask him more about Heather later, when the time was right.

"Yeah. I'll need the money by then. I can't believe I leave for college in six weeks. The summer is really going fast," he commented.

"Yes. Too fast," she said, her voice sober.

"But just think—you'll be a big-shot senior. You've waited a long time for this. You and Lori can rule the roost.

"Right," Deni said sarcastically. "We'll have a ball this year. Every Friday and Saturday night we'll baby-sit for John Christopher."

"Not planning to go out any, huh?" he asked.

"You know how it is," she said, her voice light. "Senior boys date sophomore and junior girls, and senior girls baby-sit."

"Unless they're dating college freshmen," he said.

"College freshmen date college freshwomen," she said turning toward him.

"Not all of them," he said, suddenly serious. "Not the smart ones who have a special girl back home." He kissed her lightly on the lips. "Like me," he said, looking deeply into her eyes. "I love you, Deni."

"And I love you," she whispered, putting her arms around him. Their kiss was long, lingering. At last she had been able to tell him how she felt about him, and she had never felt so happy, so at peace with herself.

"I've learned a lot the past few weeks, Mike,"

she said as they drew apart. "Some things I hope I never forget."

He looked at her questioningly. "Like what?"

"Elaine loved me enough to put me up for adoption. My folks loved me enough to make me one of the family. My grandmother's love was unconditional, and that's how I feel about John Christopher. Any kind of love should be nourished and cherished. That's also true when you find a very special guy. Because that kind of love," she whispered, her lips close to his, "is the best kind of all."